★ THE ADVENTURES OF ★
TINTIN

★ THE ADVEN

TIN

TURES OF ★ TIN

A novel by
ALEX IRVINE

Based on the screenplay by
**STEVEN MOFFAT AND
EDGAR WRIGHT & JOE CORNISH**

Based on The Adventures of Tintin series by
HERGÉ

LITTLE, BROWN AND COMPANY
New York ★ Boston

Little, Brown and Company

Hachette Book Group
237 Park Avenue, New York, NY 10017
Visit our website at www.lb-kids.com

Little, Brown and Company is a division of Hachette Book Group, Inc.
The Little, Brown name and logo are trademarks of Hachette Book Group, Inc.

The publisher is not responsible for websites (or their content)
that are not owned by the publisher.

First Edition: November 2011

ISBN 978-0-316-18579-0

10 9 8 7 6 5 4 3 2 1

RRD-C

Printed in the United States of America

CHAPTER 1

Tintin was getting his picture painted in the Old Street Market with his dog, Snowy, lying at his feet. Around them swirled the typical activity of the market on a bright sunny day. People sold everything from fruit to art to T-shirts for tourists. The cobblestones of the town square were bustling with families out enjoying the pleasant weather—unusual for Europe at this time of year.

Members of a brass band wearing red jackets were playing some kind of oompah number on a gazebo bandstand near a small Ferris wheel full of giggling children. Tintin bobbed his head to the rhythm of the music and then stopped when he remembered that he was posing for a picture.

"Very nearly there," the artist said. "I have to say, your face is familiar. Have I drawn you before?"

"Occasionally," Tintin said. His boyish face had a smattering of freckles, and his reddish-blond hair flipped up at the front in an irrepressible quiff.

"Of course, I've seen you in the newspapers. You're a reporter?"

Snowy whined at Tintin's feet. The wire fox terrier's stub of a tail twitched, and he sat up to scratch behind one of his ears. Snowy's name came from his white wiry coat. He was very smart. Sometimes Tintin thought Snowy was as smart as most people he knew. Snowy was still a terrier, though: curious, headstrong, and easily bored. It was hard to keep him sitting down long enough for Tintin to do something like get a picture painted.

"I'm a journalist," Tintin corrected him. Reporters ran around yelling for quotes. Journalists hunted down stories and unraveled clues to uncover the truth. Tintin thought this was an important distinction. "Be patient, Snowy. Not much longer."

Snowy looked up at Tintin, wanting to see the part of the

market where the food vendors gathered. There were always fine snacks to be had there. He looked around at the people, seeing mostly feet and legs and swinging bags full of market goods. Then he saw something interesting: A man was moving smoothly through the crowd, picking the pockets of the market patrons as he went. *A crime!* Snowy thought. He trotted after the pickpocket, watching as the man relieved another distracted pedestrian of his wallet.

Tintin did not notice that Snowy had left. He was concentrating too hard on sitting still, posing for his picture.

"There," the artist said at last. "I believe I've captured something of your likeness."

He showed Tintin the picture, and Tintin admired it. The artist had done a good job, he thought. Tintin looked at himself on the paper and saw his hair with the flip at the front that no amount of combing or wetting could flatten. He was wearing his tan spring overcoat over a blue sweater and a white shirt. In the picture he was looking off to the side as if he had just seen something very interesting. He looked like he was about to go off in search of mystery and adventure.

He liked it. "Not bad," he said. "Snowy, what do you think?"

Tintin looked down. Snowy was nowhere to be seen.

"Snowy...?" He looked around, wondering where his adventurous little dog had run off to. The artist cleared his throat, and Tintin handed him money for the portrait. Then he strolled through the market, keeping an eye out for Snowy, the portrait rolled up and stuck in his pocket.

He did not see that others were keeping an eye on him from a bench not far from the bandstand. Through two newspapers, each with two holes cut out of the page, two pairs of eyes tracked Tintin's progress.

Tintin heard Snowy bark from somewhere in the crowd. He stopped and called out, "Snowy!"

A stall full of mirrors for sale reflected his image in a most confusing way. He saw himself from a dozen different angles, with a dozen different backgrounds. For a moment he looked around, puzzling over which reflection to look at. Then he got his bearings. "Snowy!" he called again, turning away from the mirrors and passing a stall where an array of antiques were on display.

The salesman was one of the market's fixtures, a pipe-smoking older gentleman by the name of Crabtree. Most of what he had spread out in the stall was cheap junk, labeled as *antiques* to fool tourists. But placed in the center of the display, as if Crabtree had known it was better than the rest of his wares, was a magnificent model of a sailing ship. Snowy appeared from the crowd as Tintin bent down to get a better look at the model.

"Snowy," he said, "look at this!"

Snowy plopped down next to Tintin and tilted his head to consider the ship.

"Triple-masted, double decks, fifty guns," Tintin said. "Isn't she a beauty?"

Snowy thumped his stubby tail on the ground.

"That's a very unique specimen, that is," Crabtree said. "From an old sea captain's estate."

Tintin read the tiny lettering on its stern. "The *Unicorn*..."

"Yes, the *Unicorn*," Crabtree said. "Man-of-war sailing ship. It's very old, that is. Sixteenth century!"

Tintin could tell at a glance that the *Unicorn* was not that old. The lines were all wrong, not to mention the guns. "Seventeenth, I should think," he argued.

"Reign of Charles the First!" proclaimed Crabtree, whose descriptions of his wares were rarely based on facts.

Again, Tintin felt it necessary to correct him. "Charles the Second," he said. Charles the First had been gone long before ships of this type were built.

"That's what I said. Charles the Second," the vendor went on smoothly. Tintin had to admire his persistence. "As fine a ship as ever sailed the seven seas. You won't find another one of these, mate."

Mate? Tintin thought. Crabtree was turning into an old sea captain himself.

"And it's only two quid," Crabtree said.

Ah, Tintin thought. *Now we get to the point.* He looked down at Snowy, whose tail had stopped wagging. "I'll give you a pound," he said.

"Done!" Crabtree looked satisfied. Tintin wondered if he would have taken even less. *Ah, well, too late.*

Tintin gave him the pound note and took the wonderful model as Crabtree lifted it out of its display case and handed it over. "Easy does it," Crabtree said, being careful of the tiny rigging and masts.

"Excuse me!" a voice called out from the crowd. An American, Tintin guessed by the sound of him. As Tintin glanced over in the direction of the voice, the *Unicorn* slipped a bit in his grasp.

"Here you go, careful!" Crabtree cautioned, putting a hand out to steady it.

The source of the loud American voice proved to indeed

6

be a loud American with a black mustache, wearing a blue suit and a fedora. He shoved his way through the crowd and arrived with one hand already reaching for his pocket. "Hey, bud," he said to Crabtree, nodding at the *Unicorn*. "How much for the boat?"

"I'm sorry," Crabtree said, "but I've just sold it to this young gent."

"Oh, yeah?" the American asked. He spun and leaned in toward Tintin, crowding him aggressively. "Tell me what you paid and I'll give you double."

"Double?" Crabtree echoed, shocked. Tintin thought the vendor was pretending to be shocked at the American's poor manners, but he was actually shocked that he had missed out on a chance to make more money.

"Thanks," Tintin said, "but it's not for sale."

The American tried a different tack. He draped an arm over Tintin's shoulders, and Tintin let him, knowing that Americans were very familiar sometimes. "Look, kid, I'm trying to help you out," he said. "The name's Barnaby. I don't think you realize this, but you're about to walk into a whole mess of danger." He darted his eyes back and forth as if trying to emphasize the danger.

"Danger?" Tintin repeated. Where there was danger,

usually there were good stories as well—and as a journalist, Tintin loved nothing better than a good story.

Well, except perhaps a good story that also involved a good adventure along the way. Tintin didn't think stories were worthwhile unless they involved mysteries for him to solve. He had often stumbled upon crimes and secrets, and taken jaw-dropping risks as he investigated odd events in the name of journalism. He just couldn't resist a clue.

Before he could get anything else out of Barnaby, though, the American saw something in the crowd and a look of alarm appeared on his face. "I'm warning you—get rid of the boat and get out while you still can!" he hissed in Tintin's ear. "These people do not play nice."

"What people?" Tintin asked, but he got no answer from Barnaby's back as Barnaby melted into the market crowds.

"Wonderful!" another voice said.

Tintin turned to see a very tall, stooped man with a long black beard and a tiny pair of glasses perched on the narrow bridge of his nose. Everything about him was long and angular. His coat hung on him as if his shoulders were a coat hanger. His beard and swooping mustache ended in points. Even his tall bowler hat somehow lost its look of roundness when surrounded by so many sharp angles and lines.

Despite his thinness, he looked energetic and powerful. Perhaps this was because he was dressed in shades of red, with a crimson tie setting off the darker red of his suit and vest.

"It's just wonderful!" the man repeated, removing his hat to bend close to the ship. His hair, swept back from a high forehead, was dramatically streaked with white. "Don't bother wrapping it—I'll take it as is! Does anybody object if I pay by check?"

Crabtree cast a glance toward the skies. Tintin could tell he was wishing he'd never opened his stall that morning. "If you want to buy it," Crabtree said wearily, "you'll have to talk to the kid."

"I see," the tall man said. He put his face close to Tintin's. "Well, let the kid name his price."

That, Tintin saw, was about all Crabtree could stand. The vendor slumped in his chair. "Name his price?" he echoed in quiet despair. "Ten years I've been flogging bric-a-brac and I miss 'name your price' by one bleedin' minute!"

"I'm sorry," Tintin said. "I already explained to the other gentleman—"

The model ship's latest suitor immediately looked angry at the idea that there was another gentleman. He scanned the crowd, his bearded face darkening with a frown that teetered on the edge of a scowl.

"American, he was," Crabtree added helpfully. "All hair oil and no socks!"

Tintin had noticed his lack of socks, too. He had a hard time imagining how anyone could walk through the marketplace without socks. "It's not for sale," he said to the bearded man, a little more firmly this time.

"Then let me appeal to your better nature," came the reply. The bearded man swept his arm out in a grand gesture, though what it was intended to convey Tintin did not know. "I have recently acquired Marlinspike Hall, and this ship, as I'm sure you're aware, was once part of the estate."

"Of the late sea captain?" Tintin asked, wanting more of the story. He now thought that the strange man's gesture might have been intended to indicate the direction of Marlinspike Hall, which lay over the horizon in the hilly countryside outside of town.

"The family fell upon hard times," the bearded man said with the tone of someone repeating a story he has told many times. "They've been living in a cloud of bad luck ever since. We are talking generations of irrational behavior. It's a very, very sad story."

"I'm sorry," Tintin said. "But as I told you before, it's not for sale."

The bearded man's face contorted into an angry glare.

"Good day to you, sir," Tintin said. He nodded, made sure the model ship was secure in the crook of his elbow, and made his way into the market. Snowy, with a toss of his snout, followed.

Behind him, Tintin heard the bearded man say to Crabtree, "That young man. What's his name?"

"Him?" Crabtree said, sounding incredulous that anyone would ask such a question. "Everybody knows him. That's Tintin."

Tintin smiled to himself. *Maybe not everyone yet*, he thought. But someday everyone would know him. That much was certain.

CHAPTER 2

Tintin carried the model carefully back to his apartment on Labrador Street, on a fairly quiet block of four- and five-story apartment houses with manicured trees spaced evenly along the sidewalk. He unlocked the outside door and peered inside, hoping his landlady, Mrs. Finch, wouldn't notice him coming in. She would talk his ear off if she got the chance, and Tintin wanted to get right up to his apartment and take a closer look at the ship. He knew something about it was important because people wanted it. What he didn't know was why.

Mrs. Finch's door was closed. Tintin passed it quickly and went up the stairs to his floor, letting himself into his apartment and closing the door behind him. *Home sweet home*, he thought.

His apartment was not large, but it had everything he wanted. From the front door, the kitchen was on his left and the fireplace on his immediate right, with his favorite chair arranged in front of it. Past the fireplace, between two large windows looking out onto Labrador Street, stood his dining table. Tall bookshelves, framing the windows, occupied the corners. A door straight ahead led to Tintin's bedroom and bathroom. Another opened into his office, where his desk was stacked with books and papers from research for the stories he was currently working on. The walls were nearly covered with photographs of places Tintin had been and people he knew. It was a tidy space, perfect for him. . . . Well, it *would* have been tidy if it wasn't cluttered with the various things he had collected on his adventures. But what was the point of having adventures if they didn't result in some souvenirs?

Tintin set the model ship on his sideboard and looked down at Snowy. "What is it about this ship?" he asked, not because he thought Snowy would answer but because he liked to get his thoughts straight by talking to someone who wouldn't confuse him with answers. "Why has it attracted so much attention?"

Snowy looked at him without saying anything. Tintin leaned in close to study the model ship. "What secrets do you hold?" he asked quietly.

Snowy barked.

Of course, Tintin thought. *The magnifying glass!*

He hurried into the next room, setting his coat down on the couch and going on into his office. The room was dominated by his desk, on which his old manual typewriter sat front and center, surrounded by knickknacks and various memorabilia from his many adventures. He ran his hands over some of those things, but his mind wasn't on them; he wanted his magnifying glass.

Digging through his possessions in search of the magnifying glass, he found dozens of exotic objects and all manner of odds and ends from his various adventures, but none of them interested him at the moment.

Unable to find the magnifying glass, he stopped. He found it was always best to pause and think when he was on the verge of getting frustrated. "Where is that magnifying glass?" he said aloud, trying to remember where he'd put it. He went to his bookcase and rummaged through its shelves, finding travel guides, accounts of exploration from pole to pole and everywhere in between, clippings of articles he had published, several dried-out fountain pens, a letter written by the American gangster Al Capone...but no magnifying glass.

"Where is it?" he said again.

Snowy woofed quietly from near his feet...well, not quietly, exactly. He woofed as if something was in his mouth and he couldn't let out a full woof without dropping it. Tintin looked down.

Snowy had his magnifying glass.

"Thank you," Tintin said, taking it.

The terrier responded by turning his head away from Tintin and growling. Tintin turned, too, and saw a large white cat in the doorway. It must have come in through the window.

Oh no, he thought. Snowy sprang after it, ignoring Tintin, who called out, "No, Snowy!"

The cat skidded back into the living room, Snowy in hot pursuit. Tintin, right behind them, thought for a moment that Snowy was actually going to catch it. What would he do? Snowy, like almost every other dog Tintin had ever known, loved to chase cats. But he had never caught one, and Tintin didn't want to find out what would happen if he did.

Apparently the cat didn't want to know, either. After a couple of laps around the living room, the cat decided to go up instead of around. Leaping into the air, it caught hold of the chandelier that hung from the center of the living room ceiling. It dangled there for a moment, the chandelier swinging crazily and tinkling as Snowy barked and hopped on his hind legs. Then the cat leaped from the chandelier to the drapes, scaling them and reaching momentary safety on top of a bookshelf near the window.

But Snowy wasn't done with the chase. He wasn't a big dog, but he was determined. He jumped, snapping his jaws closed an inch from the cat's tail as the cat sprang off the bookshelf and dashed over onto the sideboard, scooting between the model ship and the wall.

Tintin saw a chance to shoo the cat out of the room. He angled in to keep the cat close to the wall, pushing it toward the window. But he heard a crash behind him, and he turned to see that Snowy had jumped up onto the sideboard after the cat...and knocked over the model ship!

Tintin spun around again. The cat was gone, back out the window. Snowy barked at the windowsill as Tintin crouched next to the ship where it had fallen on the floor. Its mast was broken off close to the base.

"Look what you did," Tintin said, holding the ship up as Snowy panted at the window, daring the cat to return. "You broke it! Bad dog!"

He examined the ship, inspecting it for other damage. It looked like the only thing wrong was the broken mast, but Tintin was annoyed. He'd just bought it and it was already broken. He set the ship back on the sideboard and gave it a second look. The mast was hollow; Tintin wondered why. Wouldn't it have been easier to use an ordinary piece of solid wood? He set the mast loosely back on its broken base, wondering if he had the right kind of glue to fix it.

Snowy, meanwhile, had forgotten all about the cat and was scooting around on the floor, chasing something. A bug, perhaps. Snowy was afraid of spiders, but he loved to chase any other kind of creature that might find its way into the apartment. Whatever it was, it had gotten under a cabinet near the sideboard and Snowy was scrabbling away under the cabinet trying to root it out.

Tintin sighed and decided to stop being upset. After all, the hollow mast had presented him with a mystery. And where there were mysteries, there were stories.

"Something happened on this ship, Snowy," he said. "And we're going to the one place that could have the answer."

He grabbed his coat from the couch and brushed cat hair from it. "Come on, Snowy."

Snowy ran out the door ahead of him and Tintin followed. Somewhere out there he would find the answer. He felt a little tingle of anticipation, the way he always did when he knew he was just beginning the hunt.

As he left, someone outside the building was watching. Sunlight glinted off the lenses of a pair of binoculars that focused carefully on the model ship, which sat on the sideboard, the mast leaning crookedly from its broken base.

Inside the Maritime Library everything was quiet. The interior looked like the inside of a ship, with dark wood everywhere and ancient cannons pointed at the windows. Staircases and ladders led to the book stacks, and lanterns hung from the walls and ceiling. Everything either had a nautical theme or looked as if it had been salvaged from a long-sunken man-of-war. Tintin could almost hear the sound of waves, the creak of timbers, the snap of sails as the wind changed direction...but in reality the only sounds were whispers. People spoke in whispers and the books whispered, too, as patrons turned their pages. Tintin sat by himself at a wide table, paging carefully through a huge leather-bound maritime encyclopedia. He was thinking of what the bearded man in the market had said about Marlinspike Hall and the ship....

Aha!

"Here it is, Snowy!" Tintin said in a low whisper. Under the table, Snowy's stubby tail thumped on the floor. Tintin read the entry. *"Sir Francis Haddock of Marlinspike Hall, the last captain of the ill-fated* Unicorn.*"*

Tintin paused to look closely at an illustration of the *Unicorn* under full sail on the high seas. It had sailed from Barbados in 1676, and was attacked by pirates shortly after leaving port. "All hands lost except for one survivor," Tintin informed Snowy, who had crept up and put his front paws on Tintin's lap so he could get a look at the book, too. Sometimes Tintin thought Snowy could even read.

Sir Francis himself had been the lone survivor, and when he returned home to Marlinspike Hall, he was convinced that the voyage had cursed his name. "A curse, Snowy," Tintin whispered. "And listen to this: *The* Unicorn's *manifesto stated that it was carrying a cargo of rum and tobacco bound for Europe. But it was long claimed the ship was carrying a secret cargo.*"

He dropped a hand to scratch between Snowy's ears. "What was the ship carrying, Snowy?"

On the next page, the entry ended: *Historians have tried and failed to discover what happened on that fatal voyage, but Sir Francis's last words hint at the difficulty of the mystery: "Only a true Haddock will discover the secret of the* Unicorn*."*

Tintin closed the book. The secret of the *Unicorn*. His pulse quickened. He might not be a true Haddock, but Tintin was willing to bet that *he* could discover that secret. He had found the first outlines of a mystery. Now he wouldn't be able to stop until he had filled in every last detail. "The secret of the *Unicorn*..." He looked down at Snowy. "What do you think?"

He heard something in the aisle behind him, but when he looked over his shoulder, the aisle was empty. Outside it had begun to rain, and the library was growing dark. Lightning flashed through the windows, throwing the shelves of old books into stark relief. Suddenly the library seemed spooky to Tintin. He felt as if he were being watched.

Tintin stood and Snowy came out from under the table. For a moment he listened, but if there was someone else in the library near him, that person was being perfectly silent. It was already a strange day, Tintin thought. *Two different people showed up the moment I bought the model. What do they want with it?* He did not believe the red-suited man's excuse about Marlinspike Hall. He also didn't know if he believed Barnaby's warnings about danger.

But clearly something was going on. Tintin felt a little thrill. "I've missed something, Snowy," he said quietly. "We need to take a closer look at that model."

He and Snowy walked quickly back home through the rain. Tintin couldn't shake the feeling that he was being watched, but he couldn't see who might be watching him. Because of the weather, the streets were largely deserted. Those few people he did see kept their heads down under umbrellas or held their collars up against the rain. None of them seemed very interested in a young man and his dog.

The puzzle of the ship preoccupied him. Something about the hollow mast was important—or was it? Was he focusing on that and missing another clue? The only way to find out was to get another look at the ship. He would sit down with the model and examine it from stem to stern. Something important would present itself.

But when he opened the door to his apartment and shook the rain from his coat, he looked over and saw Snowy's snout pointed at the sideboard.

The model ship was gone.

Strangers in the marketplace were one thing. Strangers breaking into Tintin's apartment were quite another. The time had come to take action!

The question, of course, was what action to take.

Tintin knew that the *Unicorn* model was valuable to at least two people other than himself. One was the American blowhard Barnaby. The other was the strange bearded man from the market…who had just taken possession of Marlinspike Hall.

And Marlinspike Hall had been mentioned in the encyclopedia entry on the *Unicorn*. It was the ancestral seat of the Haddocks. The red-suited man from the market was not a Haddock — of this Tintin was certain, but he was equally certain that the man had something to *do* with the Haddocks. But what?

The answer might be found at Marlinspike Hall.

A short while later, after the sun went down, he was creeping along the shadowed base of a high brick wall toward a rusted iron gate with a full moon shining in the clear sky and Snowy skulking along at his feet. His white fur appeared almost fluorescent in the moonlight. It was windy, and dead leaves rustled in the nighttime breeze. Next to the gate, a plaque, streaked from age and weather, read MARLINSPIKE HALL.

Tintin looked around. He and Snowy were a long way down a winding dirt road, far in the countryside. There was no sign of any other human presence. Tintin pushed on the gate. It didn't move. Then he pulled on it. It still didn't move.

How was he going to get in? The walls were too high to climb. Yet he had to get inside. Marlinspike Hall held the answer to the puzzle. The more he thought about it, the more certain he became.

"What do you think, Snowy?" Tintin asked — then realized that he was talking to Snowy through the gate.

Snowy was inside!

"How'd you do that?" Tintin asked him, grabbing the gate's bars and shaking them. Snowy trotted a few paces away from the gate and stuck his head into a hole in the wall, wriggling through to emerge not ten feet from where Tintin stood. He hadn't noticed the hole in the darkness. "Clever boy," he said.

He squatted in front of the hole. It looked as if he would fit. He worked his head and shoulders in, using his elbows to pull and feet to push. He could feel Snowy snuffling around his feet. When he got through, Tintin stood and brushed the earth and leaves from his clothes. Snowy appeared next to him.

Between them and Marlinspike Hall itself, the grounds were mostly open, but there were clusters of trees and undergrowth here and there. If they hopscotched from cluster to cluster, with a little luck Tintin thought he and Snowy could get close to the door without being seen. He looked up. There were a few clouds, but the moon was very bright. Not the best circumstances for sneaking around, especially for Snowy.

He took a moment to look over the main house itself now that he could really see it. Once, it had been a grand-looking place—that much was apparent. It was built in the chateau style, with stone walls and lots of windows. Various turrets gave its roof a regal appearance, as if someone mighty had piled stone on stone to create a monument to the Haddocks and their seagoing legacy. But Tintin could also see that Marlinspike Hall was falling into neglect. Vines crept up the stones, and shingles were missing from parts of the roof. The grounds were becoming a tangle of untrimmed bushes and overgrown grass. Tintin wondered what the inside looked like. With any luck he would find out soon.

Scooting quickly from tree to tree, he made a zigzag approach to the front door. Along the way he kept an eye out for light in the windows or any sign that someone might be watching from within. But Marlinspike Hall looked as if no one had lived there since before Tintin was born.

At the base of the steps leading up to the front door, Tintin decided to risk a flashlight. The first thing he noticed when he turned it on was a coat of arms carved into the arch over the doorway. It was a medieval jumble of shields and an eagle and a—was that a unicorn? And there was a fish. Tintin puzzled over it. "A coat of arms," he said softly. Sometimes when he was thinking hard, it helped him to speak out loud. "Why does that look familiar?"

Then the answer presented itself. The fish was a haddock. *Ah*, Tintin thought. *Of course*. Marlinspike Hall was the Haddock estate, and their most famous ship had been the *Unicorn*. "See, Snowy?" he said, starting to point out the elements of the coat of arms.

But just as Tintin spoke, Snowy ran off from the house. "Snowy!" Tintin called. What was he doing?

With a low growl, an enormous guard dog suddenly charged at Tintin from out of the shadows!

Tintin jumped off the side of the porch and sprinted back across the grounds in the general direction of the hole in the wall. He hurdled a fallen tree and nearly knocked himself out on a low-hanging branch. The dog was right behind him! Tintin cut through some brush, thinking it would slow down the dog, but his coat snagged. He struggled through the thicket as the great canine worked its way closer, head low and teeth bared.

Just before it could clamp its jaws on him, Tintin sprang free of the brambles and ran pell-mell toward the wall. The thicket was larger than he had thought. He ran along its edge, hoping to keep the large dog stuck in it as long as possible.

How he was going to get over the wall, though—that was going to be a trick. He glanced over his shoulder and saw that the guard dog was free of the brambles and closing in on him again. *Uh-oh*, Tintin thought. He wasn't going to make it to the wall, let alone have time to find the little hole and worm his way through it.

The dog was close enough that Tintin could hear its heavy breathing. He clutched the flashlight tightly and made a run for it.

But Snowy came to the rescue! He burst from the brambles and planted himself in the guard dog's path, head low, barking furiously. "Snowy!" Tintin called, skidding to a halt and turning back to protect his dog... but there was no need. The guard dog had also come to a skidding halt and was... cowering before Snowy? It was! It even licked Snowy's muzzle while Snowy stood stiff-legged and still growling.

Tintin couldn't believe it. A dog that big, scared of a little terrier! "Well done, Snowy," he said, coming up to pet Snowy's head. "Good boy."

He wished he knew what to call the other dog, which looked like a Rottweiler. It wore a collar and Tintin debated whether he could look at its tags. It sure didn't seem to be much of a guard dog anymore.

Just as he reached for the Rottweiler's collar, the two dogs abruptly began a chase again, but this one was playful.

They swerved and leaped through the brush and over the fallen trees, emerging out onto the lawn as Tintin watched. *Amazing*, he thought. All that guard dog needed was a little fun and it lost all of its meanness.

He took advantage of Snowy's cleverness to get closer to the house again. With all the noise from the dogs, anyone inside would know something was up—but Marlinspike Hall was still dark and quiet. Perhaps no one was there. Tintin decided that he wouldn't try the door; either it would be locked if no one was there or it would give him away too quickly if someone was. He skirted the edge of the lawn, looking for a potential window he could climb through, and found it around the side, in the shadow of a huge fieldstone chimney.

The window was latched, but Tintin flipped the latch up with his pocketknife and slowly pushed the window open. It made only a quiet creak, and he climbed into a darkened room, clicking his flashlight on again to get a better look around. The room was full of furniture covered in white sheets, with a thick layer of dust over everything and great tangles of cobwebs in every corner. The house smelled musty, as if no one had lived there in quite some time. He wanted to explore it and discover the secrets it held. If the red-suited man from the market had purchased Marlinspike Hall, surely there should be some sign of his presence. Tintin moved across the room and through a doorway into another room, nearer the front of the house. Through an archway ahead, he could see a large open space. That was the grand foyer inside the front door. It was dark and quiet.

Tintin didn't want to go out there just yet. The room he was in looked to be some kind of sitting room or study. Here, too, most of the furniture was covered, but he could discern the shapes of the different chairs, tables, and couches. Tintin caught glimpses of paintings on the walls, seascapes and portraits of Haddocks throughout the history of Marlinspike Hall. Shelves of carved wood displayed old books and antiques, including a couple of small ship models.

Getting warmer, Tintin thought. And just as he had the thought, he spotted a long, narrow shape under a sheet, with a couple of high points causing peaks and drapes just as the masts of a model ship might. Tintin reached out and lifted away the sheet in one swift motion, revealing the model *Unicorn*!

There it stood, looking good as new. "Well, well, well," Tintin said softly. "It seems we've caught our thief."

He picked up the model ship and started to turn, planning to leave Marlinspike Hall the way he had come, through the window. But as he turned, his flashlight beam fell on a hulking figure standing between him and the door! Tintin only had time to gasp before the figure raised a candlestick and conked him on the head. He sank to the floor, feeling the *Unicorn* lifted from his hands as his eyes crossed and his flashlight went out.

CHAPTER 3

Everything spun for a while, but Tintin was a hardy young man and it took more than a knock on the head to keep him down for long. He soon sat up and saw the man who had hit him. This man, holding the *Unicorn* model, was clearly the butler. He wore a white tuxedo and stood calmly, waiting the way only a long-suffering butler could. His jowly face and bulbous nose reminded Tintin of a basset hound. As Tintin gathered his wits and planned his next move, the bearded man from the market glided into the room. "Welcome to Marlinspike Hall," he said. "I see you let yourself in."

Rubbing his head, Tintin stood. "I came to retrieve my property, Mr. . . . ?"

"You may call me Sakharine," the bearded man said with a bow and a flourish. "This is my servant, Nestor. And . . . 'your property'? I'm not sure I follow you."

"Oh, I think you do," Tintin said. "This ship was stolen from my apartment just this afternoon!"

He made a grab for the *Unicorn* model, but Nestor pivoted and held it away from him. Tintin stood back, maneuvering for another grab, but Sakharine stepped forward and spoke again. "I'm afraid you're mistaken, Mr. Tintin."

"There's no mistake," Tintin said. "It belongs to me!"

He got a hand on the *Unicorn*, and Nestor, not wanting to break it, stopped pulling. The two of them stood there, each holding part of the ship, as Sakharine said, "Are you sure?"

"Of course I'm sure," Tintin said.

Sakharine nodded at Nestor, who let Tintin take the model *Unicorn*. "I took it home," explained Tintin. "I put it on a cabinet in the living room, and then Snowy chased the cat and knocked it over, and it . . ."

Tintin put a finger on the main mast, meaning to push it loose from where Sakharine had apparently glued it into place. That's how he was going to prove that this model was his . . . but the mast did not move.

"Fell," Tintin finished. Incredulous, he faced up to the reality of the situation. "This isn't my ship."

"No, indeed," Sakharine said. Nestor took the model from Tintin and replaced it on its display stand.

Confused and embarrassed, Tintin said, "I—I'm sorry. It looks identical."

Nestor picked up the sheet where Tintin had dropped it on the floor. He flipped it out and expertly settled it over the model *Unicorn* as Sakharine took Tintin by the arm and led him through the darkened house toward the front door. His cane tapped on the stone floor with every other step, but Tintin could tell Sakharine didn't really need the cane. It was only for show. "Well, looks can be deceiving," Sakharine said.

"Yes, indeed," Tintin agreed. His mind was spinning and he let himself be led—but then an idea occurred to him, and he broke away from Sakharine, heading back toward the display case to take a closer look. Nestor kept careful watch but made no move to stop him.

"But I don't understand," Tintin said. "Why did Sir Francis make two ships exactly alike? And you have one already.

Why do you want another? What is it about this model that would make someone want to steal it?"

"Goodness me," Sakharine said as he followed Tintin back into the room. "Why so many questions?"

Tintin felt that Sakharine was humoring him. "It's my job," he said. "There could be a story here. It's what I do, you see."

"Well, it's no great mystery. Sir Francis Haddock was a hopeless reprobate. He was doomed to fail and he bequeathed that failure to his sons." Again, Sakharine walked toward the front door, clearly expecting Tintin to follow him.

"So it's true!" Tintin said. "The Haddock line is cursed!"

Sakharine spun around and prodded Tintin in the shoulder with his cane, stopping him in his tracks. "What else have you found out?" he asked, his good humor suddenly gone.

Aha, Tintin thought. He was on the right track. Sakharine's response proved it. He pushed the cane away. "What is there to find?"

The cane rose up again and poked Tintin's other shoulder. "That depends on what you're looking for," Sakharine said.

"I'm looking for answers, Mr. Sakharine."

Sakharine smiled, but it was the kind of smile that made Tintin uneasy. "You're looking in the wrong place. Now, it is late. I think you should go home."

Nestor appeared and handed Tintin's flashlight back to him. "This way, sir," he said, and led the way to Marlinspike Hall's spacious foyer.

When they arrived at the front door, Nestor held it open and said, "It's a pity, sir."

Tintin, on his way out the door, stopped and turned. "I'm sorry?" he said, not understanding.

"That the mast broke on your model ship, sir. I hope you found all the pieces." Nestor lowered his voice as he went on, and he glanced back toward the room containing the second model ship. "Things are so easily lost."

"I beg your pardon?" Tintin said in a voice barely above a whisper. He didn't understand.

Nestor looked as if he might say more, but at that moment Sakharine called from within the house. "Nestor!"

Nestor gave Tintin a significant look, but Tintin still didn't know what he was getting at. He started to ask, but Nestor said, "Good night, sir," and shut the door firmly in his face. Tintin stood there for a moment, thinking over what had happened inside Marlinspike Hall. Then Snowy and his new guard-dog friend appeared, and it was time to go.

It was very late when Tintin got back to his apartment at 26 Labrador Street. He looked up and down the street, again feeling like he was being watched. The street was still wet from the storm, and the moon was lower in the sky. Everything was dark. He thought he saw shadows flitting between parked cars—and was that a human figure skulking from doorway to doorway down by the corner? The familiar scene seemed spooky now that Tintin sensed he had uncovered the beginning of a great mystery. Someone did not want him to know what had happened to the Haddocks, and did not want him to know what the secret of the *Unicorn* really was.

"Snowy," he said, "I've got myself spooked. I'm jumping at shadows."

With a last look around, Tintin unlocked the building door and went inside, determined to focus on the story. *Marlinspike Hall*, he thought. There was a mystery there. Sakharine was hiding something, and Nestor...had Nestor given him a clue? If so, why?

"Some things are easily lost," he said, thinking of Nestor's parting words. "What did he mean by that, Snowy?"

Snowy cocked his head toward the door.

"What was he trying to tell me? Some things are easily lost...."

He thought it over as they went up the stairs and into Tintin's apartment. Snowy growled as Tintin stopped to turn on the light.

"Great snakes!" he said when he saw what had happened.

His apartment had been ransacked! The furniture had been pulled away from the walls and overturned. His books had been spilled out of the shelves and lay in heaps on the floor. The table by the window had been swept clean of the books and magazines Tintin had been reading. He leaned into his office and saw more chaos. His papers lay in drifts around the drawers of his desk, which had been pulled out and emptied. His bulletin board, covered with clippings and notes, had been knocked off the wall and lay against a filing cabinet.

Who had done this? And why? They couldn't have been after the model of the *Unicorn*. It was already gone, and whoever had come in would have known that right away. Tintin stepped carefully into the mess, searching for any clues as to what the intruder might have been looking for.

Snowy whined as he picked his way through the debris...
and then he made a beeline for the cabinet where he had
been scratching earlier in the day.

"What is it, Snowy?" Tintin asked. Snowy started scratching under the cabinet again.

It couldn't be an insect, Tintin thought. Insects didn't keep
Snowy's interest for that long. If Snowy wanted Tintin to
see something that urgently, Tintin probably needed to
see it.

He moved Snowy aside and pulled the cabinet away from
the wall. Snowy barked and pushed against his legs as he
looked behind the cabinet and saw a small metal tube lying
on the floor against the wall.

"What's this?" Tintin wondered. He bent to pick it up,
and as he rolled it in his fingers, he figured it out. "Aha!
This was hidden in the hollow mast."

His pulse quickened. This was what the intruder had
wanted. Maybe whoever had stolen the *Unicorn* model had
found it was missing and come back to look for it. Or
maybe two different people were after it, and the one who
had stolen the model wasn't the same one who had tossed
his apartment.

I'll figure it out, Tintin thought. *But the first step is to see
what's in this tube.*

He went to the table and sat. Snowy bounced around the chair, trying to get a look. Carefully, Tintin unscrewed the lid of the tube and shook out a small rolled-up parchment. It fell into his palm, and he examined it before proceeding. It was tied with a piece of ribbon and also sealed with wax. There was some kind of insignia in the wax, but he couldn't tell what it was.

Tintin untied the ribbon and set it aside. Then he gingerly broke the wax seal, taking care not to tear the parchment. He heard Snowy moving around the apartment and looked up, concerned... but Snowy was bringing him his magnifying glass again.

"Good boy, Snowy," Tintin said. He was lucky to have such a smart dog.

He took the magnifying glass and unrolled the parchment, smoothing it on the tabletop. Something was written on it in an ornate script that at first he had some trouble deciphering. Then he peered through the magnifying glass and worked out the writing.

"*Three brothers joined,*" he read out loud so Snowy could hear. "*Three Unicorns in company, sailing in the noonday sun will speak. For 'tis from the light that light will dawn, and then shine forth the Eagle's Cross.*"

Tintin paused, thinking over what he had just read. Three

*Unicorn*s? He knew of two models, his and Sakharine's. Was that what the passage was talking about? Was there a third?

It could mean something else entirely, he thought. After all, none of the models could sail. Maybe there had been three ships called the *Unicorn*? But the maritime encyclopedia in which Tintin had read the story of Captain Haddock hadn't mentioned any other ships by that name.

It was a puzzle, that much was clear—and where there were puzzles there were good stories. Tintin put the magnifying glass back to his eye and looked at the rest of the parchment.

Below the writing was a series of strokes and dashes. "What are these markings, Snowy?" Tintin mused. "Some kind of secret language, or a code? It makes no sense. But it does explain why they ransacked our place." He was sure now that the people who had stolen the *Unicorn* model had come back. They were after this parchment, and they had torn his apartment to pieces looking for it. That meant it was valuable, but Tintin didn't know why. Who would want a strange poem? Who had gone to the trouble to hide it in the model in the first place? What did the strokes and dashes mean?

Someone out there knew the secret. Barnaby, perhaps? He had warned Tintin about the danger of possessing the model ship. Sakharine? He had threatened Tintin, and his butler had knocked Tintin out with a candlestick. He would certainly not hesitate to break into Tintin's apartment.

Whoever it was, Tintin thought, the intruder knew more of the story than he did. Which made him all the more determined to catch up and solve the mystery.

"We'll have to keep a close eye on this parchment, Snowy," Tintin said, reaching down to scratch his anxious dog between the ears. "Whoever is after it, we can be sure of one thing. They'll be back."

As if on cue, the downstairs doorbell jangled. Tintin jumped. Who could be visiting at this late hour? He would have to be ready for anything.

CHAPTER 4

Tintin did not know Mrs. Finch's first name or anything else about her except that she loved hot chocolate more than any other person Tintin had ever met did. He heard her voice now as he tucked the parchment into his wallet and crept quietly to the top of the stairs, eager to see who had rung the doorbell so late at night. A man said something to her, but Tintin couldn't tell who he was or what had been said.

Should he run? Should he confront the visitor? Surely this was related to the break-in, but whoever had ransacked his apartment wouldn't take the trouble to knock this time. That didn't make any sense.

So who was it, and what did he want?

"No, I don't know where he is, dearie," Mrs. Finch was saying. "I think he's gone out. And anyway it's after dark, and Mr. Tintin is most particular about not admitting visitors after bedtime."

This wasn't exactly true. Mrs. Finch was the one who didn't like people coming in at night, especially when they interrupted her while she was enjoying her hot chocolate. "I have to go back to my cocoa," she went on. "I've got a very good book and a cup of cocoa. Lovely..."

Tintin had been working his way down the stairs as she spoke. He could see that she had opened the front door just a crack, leaving the chain on. "Thank you, Mrs. Finch," he said, reaching the ground floor. "I can look after this."

She started and looked at him sourly. Mrs. Finch was a prim older woman who always wore cardigan sweaters and had no chin whatsoever. She excelled at sour looks. Tintin smiled at her, and she disappeared back into her apartment, from which Tintin could smell hot chocolate.

When her door was locked behind her, Tintin approached the front door cautiously. He had picked up his heavy flashlight as he left his apartment in case he needed a weapon to defend himself. The lump on his own head from Nestor's candlestick still hurt.

"Hey, kid," said a voice through the crack between the door and the jamb. "Is that you? Open the door!"

Then a familiar face pressed itself into the crack. It was the loudmouth American, Barnaby. "What do you want?" Tintin asked.

"Look, the game is up!" Barnaby said. "He's gonna be back!"

Tintin was about to ask who "he" was, but Barnaby kept talking, his tone urgent even though he was making an effort to keep his voice down. "Now, I knew he wanted those boats, but I swear to God I never thought he'd kill anyone over it."

"Kill? Who?" Tintin asked. "Who are you talking about?"

"I'm trying to tell you that your life is in danger!" Barnaby said. He looked back toward the street as Tintin came closer to the door.

"Answer me!" Tintin said. "Who—?"

Bang! Bang! Bang! Three gunshots sounded from the street and three holes punched through the door as Tintin threw himself to the floor and Snowy jumped halfway up the stairs in a single bound. The last bullet split the chain, and the door opened as Barnaby fell in, the front of his shirt already red with blood. His hat fell off, and Tintin picked it up.

"Mrs. Finch!" Tintin shouted. "A man's been shot on our doorstep!"

"Not again..." Mrs. Finch complained. She went on, but Tintin had no time to listen. If someone had been shot on the doorstep before, it had happened before he lived there.

"Call an ambulance!" he cried. He ran into the street and saw a blue car pulling away. Snowy charged past him and ran after the car. "No, Snowy!" Tintin commanded. Snowy stopped on the sidewalk and barked furiously.

Tintin couldn't chase the car on foot, and he had not gotten a look at its license plate. He ran back to Barnaby, who was slipping into unconsciousness. "Barnaby!" Tintin said, kneeling next to him. Barnaby clutched a newspaper. He was poking at it with one finger, but he slowly let it go as Tintin approached. "Can you hear me? Can you—"

He saw the newspaper as it fell to the stoop, and his eyes widened. A siren sounded in the distance, growing closer. Mrs. Finch had called the ambulance. The police would arrive soon as well. But at that moment, Tintin's eyes were glued to the newspaper. He picked it up carefully and started thinking about what to do when the police arrived.

Beside him, Barnaby moaned. His eyes fluttered, and he said something that sounded like "Boo."

"Steady on, Barnaby," Tintin said. "You're going to be fine."

Snowy whined and barked. The sirens drew closer. Mrs. Finch poked her head out the door. "A man shot on the doorstep," she said disapprovingly. "That's not the kind of house I want to run, Mr. Tintin."

"I understand, Mrs. Finch," Tintin said. "I can see to things from here. You don't want your cocoa getting cold."

She left him alone with the babbling Barnaby, who was waving his arms trying to stop Snowy from licking his face. "I guess you're going to be all right, Barnaby," Tintin said, "if you've got enough strength to worry about Snowy here. Easy, Snowy."

"Boo," Barnaby said, and passed out.

Bright and early the next morning, Tintin was talking to the police. The local police had come and gone, yielding the investigation to Interpol detectives Thompson and Thomson, who knew Tintin from a number of previous adventures. At first they had been suspicious of Tintin because he always seemed to turn up when unusual crimes were being committed and strange adventures were afoot. Over time, however, they had come to trust him and now they were his staunch allies.

At the moment, Thompson and Thomson were looking around at the mess in Tintin's apartment. He had stayed up half the night trying to put things in order, but it was a big job and he wasn't done yet. "The victim's name was Barnaby Dawes," Thomson said. It was difficult to tell the two men apart, but Tintin knew he was Thomson because his mustache curled outward at the tips, unlike Thompson's, which was straight.

"He was one of the top agents with Interpol," Thompson added. "But we don't have a clue what he was working on."

"Quite right," Thomson agreed. "We're completely clueless."

Very true, Tintin thought, smiling to himself. But it would have been rude to say it, so instead he asked, "Interpol doesn't have any other leads?"

"Oh, steady on, Tintin," Thomson said. "We're still filling out the paperwork."

Nodding, Thompson added, "Police work's not all glamour and guns. There's an awful lot of filing."

"Well, I might have something for you," Tintin said. He had been debating all night how much to tell them, and he had concluded that it was best to share as much information as possible. "Before he lost consciousness, the man tried to tell me something. I couldn't understand what he was saying, but then I saw this."

He held out the newspaper to Thompson and Thomson and watched their eyes widen just as his had. On the newspaper—in his own blood!—Barnaby Dawes had marked certain letters. Traced from left to right and down the page, the fingerprints spelled out:

"*Karaboudjan*," Tintin said.

"Karaboudjan," Thomson repeated.

"Yes," Tintin said. "Does that mean anything to you?"

Suddenly, Thomson snatched the paper from Tintin's hand. "Great Scotland Yard!" he cried. "That's extraordinary!"

"What is?" Tintin demanded.

Thomson waved an advertisement in Tintin's face. "Worthington's having a half-price sale on bowler hats!"

Thompson grabbed the paper from his partner. "Really, Thomson! This is hardly the time!" Then he, too, saw something on the page, and he echoed, "Great Scotland Yard!"

"What is it!?" Thomson and Tintin asked together.

"Canes are half-price, too!" Thompson said.

Tintin couldn't believe what he was hearing. A man shot on his doorstep, his model ship stolen, a strange word spelled out in bloody fingerprints! And they were talking about a sale on hats and canes.

"Are you going to take charge of this evidence?" Tintin asked.

"Positively," Thomson said. "Never fear, Tintin. The evidence is safe with us!"

He snatched the newspaper back from Thompson, rushed out the door with it, and promptly fell down the stairs. Thompson hurried out at the sound and called into the stairwell, "Thomson! Where are you?"

"Well, I'm already downstairs!" came the reply. "Do try to keep up."

Thompson stomped down the stairs after his partner. Tintin came out into the hall to see them off, and he noticed that Thomson had left the newspaper at the bottom of the stairs. He scooped it up and caught the two detectives at the front door. "Wait," he said before they could close the door behind them. "You dropped this."

"Good heavens, Thomson," Thompson said. "Look after the evidence, man."

"Sorry, Thompson," Thomson said. "My mind is on other things."

Thomson's hand went to his pocket, and Thompson said, "Ah, yes. Our light-fingered larcenist."

"What?" Tintin said. He couldn't imagine what might be more important than investigating the shooting of a fellow Interpol detective.

"The pickpocket," Thompson said. "He has no idea what's coming."

"Go on, Tintin. Take my wallet," Thomson said.

To humor his friends, Tintin reached into Thomson's pocket and pulled his wallet out of the inside pocket. It was attached to a piece of elastic that was, in turn, sewn into the pocket lining.

"Industrial-strength elastic!" proclaimed Thompson.

Tintin wondered if he should remind them they should be focused on the shooting of Barnaby Dawes. "Very, uh, resourceful," he said.

"Oh, on the contrary," Thompson said. "It was childishly simple."

50

Thomson nodded. "Simply childish. I agree."

The two detectives tipped their hats to Tintin and set off down the street. "Gentlemen," Tintin said by way of farewell.

Standing on his stoop, Tintin listened to their conversation as they strolled away and vanished into the fog. A gray morning mist hung in the air after the storm. "Mind you, I expect he's miles away by now," Thomson said.

"The pickpocket?" Thompson clarified.

"Yes," Thomson said. "I mean, knowing we're just a few steps behind him."

A gray-haired man passed between Tintin and the two detectives. Snowy growled, and Tintin knelt to hold on to him before he could follow the man and cause trouble.

"Snowy, what is it, boy?" he asked. "What do you see?"

The two detectives were now deep in a conversation about whether they should have a cup of tea. "I'd love one," Thompson was saying—just as the gray-haired man slid by and lifted the wallet out of Thomson's pocket!

The elastic stretched out as the pickpocket tried to drop the wallet into his own jacket, and at the tug, Thomson looked up, shocked. Quickly, his surprise turned to glee. "I've got you now!"

But it was not going to be that easy. The pickpocket

stretched the elastic all the way, pulling Thomson off balance, and then he let the wallet go. It snapped back into Thomson's face, and the pickpocket ran for it.

Thompson gave chase, but he tripped over the loose elastic, sprawling onto the ground and in the process stretching the wallet out to snap Thomson again! Thomson fell to the ground as his partner ran after the pickpocket, calling out, "Stop in the name of the law!"

He caught up to the pickpocket and grabbed his shoulder, but the pickpocket shrugged out of Thompson's grasp, leaving his coat behind. The coat flipped up over Thompson's face, and the detective went careening into a lamppost, knocking himself flat, just as Thomson got up and joined the chase. Thomson stumbled over Thompson, and both of them landed in a tangle at the base of the lamppost. The pair of them were hopeless!

"What's going on down there?" Tintin wondered aloud. He heard some of the ruckus, but the thick fog was blocking his view. "Come on, Snowy!" he said, and ran down the street toward the Interpol detectives. Along the way he brushed past an old man hurrying away from the scene, looking panicked at the intrusion of chaos into the quiet street. He wore round wire-rimmed spectacles and an orange tie knotted tightly around an old-fashioned, starched collar.

"I beg your pardon," the old man said, touching his hat.

"Sorry, sir!" Tintin called over his shoulder as he arrived at Thompson and Thomson, who were just getting to their feet.

"The pickpocket, Tintin!" Thomson said. "He's getting away!"

With a flash of dread, Tintin realized whom he had bumped into on the way to help the detectives. He reached into his own pocket and found it empty. "My wallet! It's gone!"

He turned back in the direction the old man had fled. "Come on, Snowy! After him!"

Running through the fog, Tintin cried out, "Stop!" He ran across the street and narrowly dodged a car that had not seen him. Brakes squealed and the sudden glare of head-lights disoriented him. Another car bore down on him as he scrambled out of the way of the first. With a yelp, Snowy jumped safely to the curb, but Tintin slipped on the slick street stones.

Suddenly, his arms were caught, and he was dragged onto the sidewalk as another car roared by, its horn blaring.

Thompson and Thomson broke Tintin's fall, and he realized they had pulled him out of the car's way with their canes.

"Steady on," Thompson said, but Tintin was already looking around to see which way the pickpocket might have gone. He had to get his wallet back — the vital parchment was inside!

"I've lost him!" He turned to the detectives. "You must find my wallet! It's very important. I have to get it back."

"And you will," Thompson said soothingly. "Leave it to the professionals."

"Stay here, Tintin," Thomson put in. "Or better yet, go home. We'll contact you when we've gotten him."

Tintin knew that would be best, but part of him wanted to give chase. He couldn't go on without that parchment. It was a critical part of the story. Nevertheless, he headed home, walking slowly at first but then picking up speed as his resourceful mind dealt with the loss of his wallet. He began to form a plan.

"We've lost the scroll, but we haven't lost the story," he told Snowy, who paced him along the sidewalk. "*Karaboudjan*. That's an Armenian word. That's our lead, Snowy." He kept thinking as he kept walking, going over everything that had happened since Nestor had escorted him from Marlinspike Hall the night before. "What was Barnaby Dawes trying to tell us when he said our lives were in danger?"

He broke off as he and Snowy approached his apartment building. Two deliverymen in coveralls were carrying a large wooden crate from a red delivery van toward the front door, which was open. Mrs. Finch must have let them in.

As Tintin and Snowy got to the door, another workman appeared in the hallway. "Mr. Tintin? Delivery for you."

Tintin looked back at the crate, which the two men were bringing closer to the doorway. It didn't look like it would even fit through the door. "But I didn't order anything," he said, and he was about to turn back toward the third workman when a handkerchief was clapped over his mouth and nose.

"Well," the workman said, "that's because it's you that's getting delivered." Tintin struggled for a moment, but there was a heavy, sweet smell and he had already breathed in whatever soaked the handkerchief. He felt himself falling, and then he blacked out completely. The last thing he heard was Snowy barking.

CHAPTER 5

The deliverymen quickly packed the unconscious Tintin in the crate and hauled it back toward the van. The word KARABOUDJAN was visibly stenciled on the side of the crate. "Quick!" the third workman was saying as he put the soaked handkerchief back in his pocket. "Get him in the van!"

Snowy was watching all of this from the sidewalk, where he had scooted out of the way of the crate. But now was the time when a dog had to take action! He sprang forward and sank his teeth into the third workman's leg. The other two already had loaded the crate containing Tintin into the van. They looked up as the third yowled in pain.

"Get off me, you confounded mutt!" he yelled, shaking Snowy off into the hallway. Snowy landed and spun across the slick floor before scrabbling to his feet and charging again—but the workman slammed the door in his face.

Snowy heard the van's engine start outside, and he knew he didn't have much time. He ran up the stairs and into Tintin's apartment, leaping up onto the desk and bracing his front paws on the windowsill. If it was good enough for a cat, Snowy figured, it was good enough for a dog.

The workman he'd bitten was getting into the van as it pulled away from the curb, out of Snowy's jumping range. He whined anxiously and tensed as another truck approached. Could he do it?

He sprang out the window as the truck was about to pass. It was a fire truck, and Snowy landed between two rungs on the ladder laid across its roof. Crouching against the wind, Snowy kept an eye on the van, which was just in front of the fire truck. He would have to be ready to jump off if it turned.

But it didn't turn right away. Instead, it suddenly slammed on its brakes. The fire truck followed suit, its brakes squealing as the sudden slowdown shook the ladder loose. The ladder shot forward, extending out over the van, taking the surprised Snowy with it. He tumbled from the ladder right onto the van's hood. Inside, the three workmen gaped at him. He tried to keep his footing on the slick hood, but the van swerved and Snowy was thrown off onto the street.

He rolled a couple of times and came up running. Ahead of him, the van was turning toward the waterfront—Snowy could tell by the forest of cranes that sprouted around the docks. He jumped from the street onto the low trunk of a passing coupe. The driver shouted at him, and he hopped from the coupe to the basket of a nearby bicycle, whose rider also yelled at him. Snowy barked, but the rider didn't understand him the way Tintin did. He looked out over the basket and saw the van getting farther away—and the bicycle was slowing down!

Again he jumped down to the street and ran at top speed toward the docks, cutting through a pen full of cows. He had to zigzag sharply through the forest of legs and hooves. The cows lowed and shied away from him, making it a dangerous trip. Snowy had a brief urge to herd them, but he put it aside. He had to find Tintin!

Emerging from the cattle pen, he came out onto the docks and saw the crate containing Tintin being loaded onto an enormous cargo ship. Snowy slowed and tried to keep out of sight, scooting from a canvas-covered stack of crates to an abandoned car to a coil of rope nearly as big as

58

the car. He watched the crate disappear into the ship and whined, trying to figure out how he could get aboard.

The loading ramp was out of the question. There were too many people watching. He looked up and down the dock, growing more and more anxious. *There!*

Bursting from his cover, Snowy ran across the dockside railroad tracks to one of the mooring pillars at the edge of the dock. The rope looped around it was so thick that it would have taken him a month to chew through it. He jumped to the top of the pillar and tiptoed up the gently curving rope before making a final jump onto the upper deck. Below, one of the crewmen on the ramp shouted. Snowy looked down and saw the crewman pointing at him. *Uh-oh*. He had to hide again.

He dashed across the deck and disappeared into the ship's superstructure, pausing for a breath once he got to a quiet, dark place where no one would think to look for him.

Tintin was on the ship, and so was he. Now all Snowy had to do was find him.

Tintin woke up slowly, confused because he was inside, someplace, and the last thing he remembered was talking to a deliveryman standing on his front stoop. He thought he heard the deliveryman's voice. He cracked one eye open with effort as the deliveryman said, "Eh, not here. Your side, Tom."

Hands rummaged roughly through Tintin's pockets and pulled at his coat. "Nothing," Tom said.

"Get that pocket," the first man said.

"I've looked at this one already, Allan," Tom said. "I'm sure of it."

Tom and Allan, Tintin thought. *Now we all know each other.* He was starting to feel almost awake again. "Have a look in his socks," Allan said, and Tom did. Tintin's foot twitched as Tom accidentally tickled him.

Tintin rolled to one side. He couldn't move his arms. Aware of a movement, he looked up and saw Sakharine, hatless but still wearing his red suit, approaching from a steel doorway. Looking around, Tintin put it all together. He was on a ship, below deck. He sat up and noted more details. His hands and feet were bound, and he was in a cage, probably in the ship's hold. Light slanted down from a couple of portholes. Beyond their small pools of illumination, he could see the vague outlines of stacked crates and other cargo. Tintin filed all of it away, trying to keep a level head even though the situation was fairly dire. Who knew what might come in handy when it was time to escape?

The two thugs who had searched him now stood waiting for Sakharine to give them some kind of direction. Allan was tall with hefty jowls, his face set in what seemed like a permanent frown beneath a leather captain's cap. Tom was more heavyset, with a tweed cap and a few days' black stubble darkening his cheeks and chin. Both wore heavy sweaters. Tom's sweater was blue, while Allan's was gray.

"Have you found it?" Sakharine demanded.

"Doesn't have it," Allan said.

"It's not on him, boss," Tom agreed. "It's not here."

"Not here? Then where is it?"

"Where's what?" Tintin asked. He felt that since they were talking about him, he ought to take part in the conversation. Plus he was beginning to shake off the aftereffects of whatever Allan had used to knock him out back at Labrador Street.

Sakharine banged the bars of the cage with his cane, making Tintin and the two henchmen wince. The sound echoed through the hold, amplified by the metal walls and floor. "Oh, I am tired of your games," Sakharine growled. "The scroll, from the *Unicorn*. A piece of paper like this."

He showed Tintin a curled bit of parchment nearly identical to the one that Tintin hoped was still in his stolen wallet. "You mean the poem," Tintin said.

"Yes!" Sakharine cried.

"The poem written in Old English."

"Yes."

"It was inside a cylinder," Tintin said.

"Yes."

"Concealed in the mast."

"Yes," Sakharine said through gritted teeth.

Tintin finally shrugged. "I don't have it."

Sakharine snapped his cane through the bars of the cage. Tom caught hold of the end, and as Sakharine pulled, a long, thin sword emerged from the cane. With a flick of his wrist, Sakharine pressed the tip of the sword into Tintin's cheek.

Uh-oh, Tintin thought. He had enjoyed playing the joke on Sakharine, but now it didn't seem like such a good idea.

"You know the value of that scroll," Sakharine said. "Why else would you take it?"

Tintin realized something then. He did not fear Sakharine. If Sakharine had wanted Tintin dead, he would already be dead. And as long as he knew something Sakharine didn't—in this case, the location of the parchment—Sakharine would have to keep him alive.

"Two ships, two scrolls," Tintin said. "Both part of a

puzzle. You have one, you need the other. But that's not it. There's something else."

Now he was trying to draw Sakharine out. Tintin was a journalist and knew how to talk to people. There was a story here, and he wanted to know what part Sakharine played.

And even if he never got a story out of it, how could he resist the mystery?

Sakharine leaned in to press against the bars, holding the point of his sword to Tintin's face. "I will find it, with or without your help," he said menacingly. "You need to think about exactly how useful you are to me."

He stood up straight again, sheathing his sword and latching the cage. Then he used his cane to tap his way toward the door as Tom and Allan followed. "Stay the course!" Sakharine ordered. "We'll deal with him on the way."

The three villains left, muttering to one another and slamming the door behind them—but just as they were shutting it, Snowy shot through the gap into the hold! He ran toward Tintin as the booming sound of the door being locked and bolted echoed through the chamber.

"Snowy!" Tintin said. He looked toward the door, making sure that neither Sakharine nor his goons had noticed.

Snowy slipped through the bars and licked his face. "It's good to see you, too. See if you can chew through these ropes."

Snowy started gnawing at the knots near Tintin's wrists, and Tintin started to formulate a plan. He wasn't going to have much time; if Sakharine's thugs returned, Tintin was sure he would never leave the ship alive.

CHAPTER 6

Sakharine stomped furiously up the stairs, pausing on a catwalk between the stairwell and his cabin door to make sure Tom and Allan knew what would be required. The huge tanker ship, named the *Karaboudjan*, rolled on the stormy seas, but no storm could match Sakharine's temper when cocky adventurers meddled with his plans. He wished they were on a pirate ship so he could make someone walk the plank. Curse it, though—he needed the lad to talk first. He could walk the plank later, or suffer some other doom of Sakharine's invention. There could be no question of Tintin leaving the *Karaboudjan* alive, and

Sakharine was also determined to make the lad reveal the secret of the scroll's location.

Whatever it took.

"He's lying," Sakharine said to Tom and Allan. "He must have the scroll. The question is, what has he done with it?"

"We searched him all over, boss," Tom said.

"I want you to go back down there and make him talk," Sakharine said, emphasizing the last three words by poking his cane into Tom's chest. "Do what it takes. Break every bone in his body if you have to."

Tom looked upset. "That's nasty," he said.

Sakharine rolled his eyes. It was hard to find good goons these days. "You know the stakes," he said. "You know what we're playing for. Just do it!"

He was about to dismiss them when another crew member, Pedro, came running up, calling Sakharine's name. He looked panicked. "Mr. Sakharine!" he said. "All *infierno* has broken loose! It's a disaster! The captain has come around—"

"What?" Allan interjected. Sakharine was equally surprised. He never expected the *Karaboudjan*'s real captain would awaken before the end of the voyage.

"He's conscious!" Pedro insisted. "He's accusing you of mutiny! He says you turned the crew against him."

66

"Sounds like he's sobered up again," Allan said, which was also what Sakharine was thinking.

"Well, don't just stand there, you fool," Sakharine said. "Get him another bottle."

"*Sí, señor,*" Pedro said. Allan and Tom both chimed in, "Yes, sir!"

Shaking his head over the quality of his henchmen, Sakharine stomped into his cabin and slammed the door. He did not wish to be disturbed until someone brought him news that Tintin had told them where the parchment was hidden.

It took only a few minutes for Snowy to chew through the ropes binding Tintin, and after that it was easy to flip the latch on the cage where Sakharine's goons had put him. But getting out of the hold? That looked to be a trickier proposition. Tintin looked around the hold, peering into the shadowy crevices between stacks of crates for any kind of tool, or something he could put to use.

"A crowbar, Snowy," he said, finding one left behind a stack of crates stenciled with Chinese characters. "That's something, perhaps."

He took the crowbar and worked it into the wheel that controlled the deadbolt on the door, jamming it tight. If he couldn't get out, at least he could make sure that Sakharine couldn't get in. Then he pulled the top off a nearby crate and propped it up so it covered the steel door's small window. As he did this, he heard a growl from somewhere in the hold. "Snowy?" he said.

But it wasn't Snowy. Snowy, in fact, was sniffing at a particular crate, and the growl was coming from inside it. *Hmmm*, thought Tintin. What sort of strange cargo was this ship carrying? He filed the question away in case it came in handy later. Right now, however, he needed that crate simply to stand on.

He pushed it over to the nearest porthole and climbed on top of the crate so he could pry the porthole open. Snowy jumped up next to him and tried to peer out the porthole, but Tintin wouldn't let him. "Not yet, Snowy. Let me see what's out there first."

With a grunt, Tintin opened the porthole. A gust of cool, salty air blew in, and he inhaled deeply. He loved the sea. He didn't like being kidnapped and caged, though. And he especially didn't like being threatened.

Leaning out the porthole, he saw that the ship was huge,

an almost endless wall of steel hull receding fore and aft. He could see the name of the ship painted on the hull: *Karaboudjan*. Tintin wasn't even surprised as the connection was revealed. Barnaby *had* tried to warn him. At least one mystery was solved.

The ocean stretched endlessly toward the horizon, rough and tumbling and gray. He was a fair distance above the water, but when he looked up, he saw that he was a fair distance below the main deck, too.

At first it seemed that there was nowhere Tintin could even think about escaping to. Then he took another look and began to consider the row of portholes directly above his. Perhaps...

A clank and a groaning sound from the door made Tintin jump. He looked back and saw that the crowbar was holding where he had wedged it into the wheel. The wheel turned a little back and forth, and Tintin heard voices from the other side, out in the hall. "Jiggle it a little bit," Tom was saying. "It's just stuck."

There was a smack and a yelp from Tom. "It's not stuck, you idiot!" Allan said. "He's bolted it from the inside."

Tintin knew he would have to act fast now that they knew he had removed the ropes that were binding him. He started looking around the room to see what else might be of use. "So you want to play it like that, do you?" Allan called from outside. "Tintin!"

Tintin didn't answer.

Then he heard Allan say, "Get the dynamite."

Uh-oh, Tintin thought. Now he was *really* going to have to move fast. "Broken crates, rope, champagne," he said, looking around. "What else do we have, Snowy?"

Snowy growled at whatever was in the crate Tintin had pushed over to the porthole. An answering growl came from within and Snowy backed away.

"There are other ways to open this door, Tintin!" Allan roared from the hall. "They'll be swabbing the decks with your innards when we're done with you!"

Points for originality, thought Tintin. But he doubted his innards would be very useful in getting the decks clean. He pushed a crate of champagne away from a corner and positioned it directly in front of the door, perhaps ten feet away. He tipped the crate on its side so all the bottles were aimed at the door, then carefully—very carefully—worked the top off the crate. Part one of the plan was in place, but it wouldn't do any good if he couldn't make part two work.

He started breaking up an empty crate. Allan was yelling

at someone to hurry up, and a hubbub of voices out in the hall told Tintin that more of Sakharine's goons were gathering.

Something thunked against the door. Tintin guessed it was those explosives Allan had mentioned. "This had better work, Snowy," Tintin said, and went back to the porthole, dragging with him a number of planks tied together and tethered to a long rope fashioned from shorter pieces of rope tied together. He fed the planks out the porthole and then the rope until the whole string of them was twisting and waving in the wind.

He leaned back into the hold to check on Snowy and see that the rest of his arrangements were in place. Everything looked about right. Then he started smelling the scent of a burning fuse.

"Here we go," Tintin said. He started to swing the length of knotted-together rope back and forth, building momentum, until he let the planks at the end fly straight up toward an open porthole above him. The bundle of planks went up, up... and missed!

And then, before Tintin could duck out of the way, the planks came straight back down and conked him right on the head, exactly where Nestor had hit him with the candlestick.

Tintin saw stars, but he was able to hold on to the rope. This was no time to be knocked out! If Allan and Tom got into the hold, Tintin wasn't ever going to wake up again.

He took a couple of deep breaths. Behind him, on the floor, Snowy whined. Everything was quiet out in the hall. Tintin figured that the henchmen were all hiding away from the impending explosion. He hefted the planks, waited as they banged off the hull of the ship below him near the churning waterline, and then tossed the bundle up again.

The rope extended and looped away from the ship in the wind, and Tintin snapped his wrist to arc the planks toward the porthole above him. He almost overbalanced and fell out the porthole. Behind him, Snowy grabbed his pants leg and held on.

The snap of Tintin's wrist sent the planks right through the porthole above, and then he yanked on the rope to twist them against the window. It worked! The planks turned and functioned as an anchor to the porthole above, and Tintin now had a rope he could climb up to safety.

And that was when the bomb went off.

CHAPTER 7

Out in the hallway, Allan and the rest of the goons stood up, guns in hand. "Move!" Allan yelled. Everyone's ears were ringing, but they could tell what he was saying by the way he waved. "Let's go!"

The men started to charge into the hold to look for Tintin, but everything was hidden by the smoke from the explosion. It had blown the door right off its hinges and left debris all over the immediate area, and right as they stepped through the doorway, they heard gunshots!

All of them ducked behind the fallen door or around the

edges of the doorway. "He's got a big shooter!" Tom said. He jumped out, brandishing his gun, and was hit and knocked down. Rolling around, he moaned, "Got me. . . ."

Then they all noticed the champagne cork that fell onto the floor next to him. Allan picked it up. "Hold your fire," he said, and peered around the edge of the door frame.

Rows of champagne bottles were aimed at the doorway. Many of them had popped their corks from the vibrations of the explosion. Foamy champagne spilled from the open bottles into a widening puddle on the floor. Allan didn't see Tintin anywhere.

Tom stuck his head out next to Allan. "He ain't here!" he said. "He's vanished!"

The sound of his voice shook loose a couple more corks. One of them ricocheted off the fallen door, and another nailed Tom square in the forehead, knocking him out cold.

Allan looked down at him for a moment, unable to quite believe what was happening. How could they all have been outsmarted by a kid they'd left tied up in a locked hold? "He's hiding," Allan said. He ducked another popping cork, which shot past him into the hall. "Search the ship!"

Tintin heard some of this as he dangled from the rope, trying to brace his feet against the ship's hull so he could climb. He couldn't help laughing at the champagne corks. Snowy, hanging by his teeth from the cuff of Tintin's pants, didn't see what was so funny. Tintin got his feet braced and pulled them up so he was leaning away from the hull. He held on with one hand and reached down with the other to help Snowy.

Once Snowy had his teeth on Tintin's jacket and his back feet hooked into Tintin's belt, Tintin started climbing. It took only a minute for him to get to the next porthole above. He reached one arm in and got himself arranged so the bottom lip of the porthole was wedged between his elbow and his side. Then he boosted Snowy into the stateroom, which was warmly lit. There was a smell of whiskey and wool inside.

Tintin followed Snowy in through the porthole and saw they were entering what must have been the captain's cabin. It was a dark-paneled room, chock-full of seagoing knickknacks and bric-a-brac. Sextants, models, charts, strange skulls and artifacts, a birdcage in which a parrot turned a single beady eye toward these strange intruders...and in the middle of it all, lying flat on his face, was a man who could only have been the captain himself. Around him were the pieces of a chair he had apparently fallen on, either because of the explosion or after dodging the planks that had come flying in through the window.

Tintin made a mental note to apologize for the planks. He was sure the captain would understand.

Unless, of course, the captain was in league with Sakharine; then they would be at odds. Tintin wasn't sure what to think yet. As he crawled in through the porthole, his foot caught on part of the rope and he fell. He sprawled on the floor, barely missing Snowy, who glanced over at him briefly and then looked back at the captain with a curious expression on his furry face.

The captain stirred and began to sit up. Tintin got a good look at him for the first time. The captain had a blunt and honest face with a big red nose and a bushy black beard. He straightened the collar of his blue wool turtleneck sweater, which he wore under a black wool coat. Unruly hair stuck out from under his gold-braided cap. He resettled the cap on his head, rubbing the spot where the plank had apparently hit him.

Then he saw Snowy, sitting on the cabin floor watching him, and the captain rocketed to his feet, punching his head straight through the floor of the birdcage so he was suddenly wearing it like a mask. "Arggghhh!" he cried. "The giant rat of Sumatra!"

In the next moment he saw Tintin, who was just getting to his feet. "Aha!" the captain said. He snatched up one of the broken chair legs and shifted into a swordsman's posture, holding the chair leg out at an angle toward Tintin. "Thought you could sneak in here and catch me with me trousers down, eh?"

Snowy growled and lowered his head, offended by being compared to a rat. Tintin got hold of another chair leg and brought it up just in time to parry a lunge from the captain. They circled each other, the captain hacking wildly at Tintin, who jumped and dodged out of reach. From the top of a sea chest, Tintin said, "I'd rather you kept your trousers on, if it's all the same to you."

"I know your game," the captain snarled. "You're one of them!"

Tintin parried a thrust and hopped back to the floor. "I'm sorry?"

"They sent you here to kill me, eh?" the captain said. Snowy lunged and caught the captain's pants leg in his teeth, shaking hard enough to unbalance the captain for a moment.

"Look, I don't know who you are," Tintin began, but the captain's rant went on.

"That's how he planned to bump me off. Murdered in my bed by a baby-faced assassin! And his killer dog!"

"Assassin?" Tintin said. "Look, you've got it all wrong." He parried yet again. "I was kidnapped by a gang of thugs."

The captain stopped and glared at Tintin. "The filthy swine!" he said. "He's turned the whole crew against me!"

"Who?"

"A sour-faced man with a sugary name," the captain growled, as if pronouncing a curse. "He bought them all off. Every last man!"

"Sakharine!" said Tintin. Now he understood what was happening aboard the *Karaboudjan*.

"Nobody takes my ship!" the captain raged.

"Sshhhh," Tintin said. He pointed toward the door. The captain appeared to understand.

He slumped against a case filled with nautical relics, suddenly feeling sorry for himself. "I've been locked in this room for days," he groaned, "with only whiskey to sustain my mortal soul."

You're certainly well sustained, then, Tintin thought, as it was clear the captain had been drinking. But it would have been rude to say it. On a whim, just to be sure, Tintin tried the door.

It opened. Tintin looked back at the captain, arching one eyebrow.

"Oh," the captain said. "Well, I assumed it was locked."

"Well, it's not," Tintin said. "Now you must excuse me. If they find me here, they'll kill me. I have to keep moving and try to find my way off this drunken tub."

He slipped out into the corridor with Snowy, shutting the door behind him and walking straight into a sailor he hadn't seen coming. A guard, or someone just passing by? It didn't matter. The sailor caught Tintin in a bear hug and they wrestled as, from inside the cabin, Tintin heard, "Tub? Tub!? *Tub!??*"

The door opened just as Tintin and the sailor spun around in the corridor, banging into the wall next to it. In a rage, the captain knocked the sailor down with a single punch. He fell to his hands and knees, trying to get up. When he lunged for the captain's legs, the captain slammed the door into him, knocking him out cold. Tintin caught the sailor as he fell over and, with the captain's help, dragged him into the cabin.

"Thanks," Tintin panted when they had laid the sailor out.

"Pleasure," the captain said.

Tintin offered his hand. "I'm Tintin, by the way."

The captain shook Tintin's hand. "Haddock. Archibald Haddock. There's a longboat up on deck. Follow me."

With that, he went into the corridor. Tintin did a double take as he registered what the captain had said. He couldn't believe it! Had he narrowly escaped death only to stumble right into the cabin of the one man on Earth who could unlock the secret of the *Unicorn*?

"Hang on a second," he called, hurrying after the captain with Snowy right at his heels. "Did you say *Haddock*?"

CHAPTER 8

On the bridge, Allan and Tom were weathering a storm. Not from the ocean, which was beginning to calm a bit, but from Sakharine, who was enraged at Tintin's escape.

"Champagne bottles!" he roared. "You hid from champagne bottles. You let the boy escape and now Haddock is out, too? Because the boy climbed the outside of the ship? Find them! Find them both!"

"Don't worry, we'll kill 'em, sir," Allan said.

"No. You can kill the boy. Not Haddock," Sakharine

said. He tapped Allan with his cane to make sure Allan got the message.

"Oh, he's just a hopeless old drunk," Tom said. "We shoulda killed him long since."

Now it was Tom's turn to take a couple of pokes from Sakharine's cane. "You think it's an accident that I chose Haddock's ship, Haddock's crew?" Sakharine demanded. Looking back at Allan, he added, "Haddock's treacherous first mate? Nothing is an accident."

He let the tip of his cane fall back to the floor and looked out to sea as Allan and Tom exchanged perplexed glances. Wind ruffled his hair and beard, and as Sakharine raised his arm, his hunting falcon spiraled down out of the sky and landed on his forearm. "We go back a long way, Captain Haddock and I. We have unfinished business, and this time I'm going to make him pay."

Tintin followed Captain Haddock through the maze of the *Karaboudjan*'s lower decks. They stopped every so often to wait for running footsteps to pass as the crew searched for them. "We have to reach the door at the end of this corridor and up the stairs," Haddock said as they peered around a corner down a long stretch of hallway with no cover. "This is going to be tricky."

Indeed it was, Tintin thought. Despite the urgent situation, though, he couldn't help asking questions. "You wouldn't happen to be related to the Haddocks of Marlinspike Hall, would you?"

Haddock squinted at him. The question made him wary, Tintin could tell. "Why do you ask?"

"It's for a story I've been working on," Tintin said. "An old shipwreck that happened off the coast of Barbados. A man-of-war, triple-masted, fifty guns."

Before Tintin could say more, Haddock grabbed him by the shirtfront and slammed him up against the wall. "What do you know of the *Unicorn*?" he hissed.

"Not a lot," Tintin said. "That's why I'm asking you."

This answer appeared to calm Haddock somewhat. "The secret of that ship is known only to my family. It has been passed down from generation to generation. My granddaddy himself with his dying breath told me the tale." Haddock's gaze grew distant as he reminisced.

Tintin waited for a moment, then prompted him. "And?"

"Gone," Haddock said, shaking his head.

"What do you mean, gone?"

"I was so upset when he kicked the bucket, I had no choice but to drown me sorrows," Haddock said sadly. The whiskey on his breath told the rest of the story. "When I woke up in the morning...it was gone. I'd forgotten it all."

"Everything?" Tintin said. He was stunned. At first it had seemed like an incredible stroke of fortune that he had escaped from the hold straight into the cabin of the one man who would have known the secret of the *Unicorn.* Now he was downcast, because Captain Haddock's memory was lost to drink and Tintin was right back where he had started. In fact, he was worse off. Sakharine was probably very unhappy that Tintin had escaped.

"Every last word." Haddock looked up and down the corridor. The coast was clear, and he took off toward the stairs that led up to the door that was their goal. Tintin followed, still not quite able to believe that Haddock had forgotten *everything.*

He couldn't give up so quickly. "Well, is there somebody else in your family?" he asked. "Maybe they would know."

"Sir Francis had three sons," Haddock said. "All but my bloodline failed. I am the last of the Haddocks."

Here is a possibility, Tintin mused, thinking of the poem

from the parchment. A thin one, but it was all he had. "Did you say *three* sons?"

They got to the bottom of the stairwell just as a search party entered the stairwell on the floor above. Haddock, Tintin, and Snowy ducked under the stairs and froze as the sailors passed. Snowy couldn't help himself. He let out a small whimper after they were gone. Tintin patted him on the head to soothe him.

Haddock came out, looked around, and started up the stairs. Tintin and Snowy followed. *Three sons*, Tintin was thinking... and just like that, he had it.

"I know what Sakharine's looking for!" he said in a too-loud whisper just as they reached the top of the stairs.

Haddock whirled to shut him up. "What are you raving about?"

"It was written on the scroll," Tintin said. *"Three brothers joined. Three Unicorns in company sailing in the noonday sun will speak."*

Amazed, Haddock just gaped at Tintin for a long moment. Then he said, "Really?"

"Sir Francis didn't make two models of the *Unicorn*. He made three! Three ships for three sons!" Tintin felt a rush of excitement at solving this part of the puzzle.

Haddock appeared to feel it, too. "Excellent!" he said, and headed off down the corridor with a new spring in his step.

"Sakharine's after the third model ship," Tintin said.

They reached a door and Haddock tried it. It wouldn't open. "Barnacles!" Haddock swore. "Someone's locked the door!" He stood there, apparently at a loss for what to do next.

Tintin wanted to talk about the three models, but Captain Haddock's mind was elsewhere. What a frustrating man he was! "Is there a . . . key?" Tintin suggested.

"Key!" Haddock said. "Yes! Now that would be the problem."

Again he led Tintin through the convoluted mid-decks of the *Karaboudjan*, and again they hid and dodged search parties. After a few minutes they arrived at a door just like the locked door at the other end of the ship, but this one was open just a crack. Haddock pushed it slowly and carefully. His body language told Tintin that they must remain absolutely silent.

The two of them peered into the room beyond the door, Snowy also taking a look and sniffing the air. It was dark and the sounds of snoring were Tintin's first indication of where they were. His eyes adjusted to the gloom, and he saw a motley group of sailors sleeping, sprawled in hammocks and bunks and on the floor.

"Mr. Jaggerman," Haddock whispered. "Top bunk in the center. Keeper of the keys. Careful, mind; he's a restless sleeper on account of the tragic loss of his eyelids."

"He lost his eyelids?" Tintin said. How was he going to sneak up on a man with no eyelids?

"Aye," Haddock said. "Now that was a card game to remember." For a moment he was lost in thought. Then he shook himself out of his reverie. "I'd do this myself, Tintin, but you've a lighter tread and less chance of waking the boys."

Tintin was not at all convinced. "Are you sure this is a good idea?"

"You've nothing to worry about," Haddock said.

The ship began to roll as Tintin squatted to give Snowy a little scratch under the chin and tell him to stay put. The ship must have been entering rougher seas again. *What luck*, Tintin thought. *Just as I have to tiptoe among sleeping sailors to lift a set of keys from a man with no eyelids, the floor starts to move. I might as well have stayed tied up in the hold!*

But there was not much choice, so he set off down the narrow aisle between the rows of bunks and hammocks. He could see the bunk Haddock had pointed out. He could even see the faint gleam of the keys in Mr. Jaggerman's hand.

"Provided," Haddock added helpfully, "they all stay asleep."

Yes, Tintin thought. *That would help.*

He waved back at Haddock to hush him but teetered at the pitch of the floor. Haddock saw the motion and misunderstood it. "Don't!" he whispered, too loudly. "I wouldn't get too close to Mr. Hobbs. He's very handy with a razor." Haddock kept up with the hoarsely whispered advice as Tintin crept on, dodging the sleeping sailors who moved about constantly. They got in his way, rolled out of their bunks, got up and stumbled to other bunks—all without waking. Tintin had never seen a group of people sleep so deeply.

He got to Mr. Jaggerman's bunk and looked up. He would have to climb to reach it; the bunks were stacked four high, and the highest of them was well beyond Tintin's reach even if he stood on tiptoes. He glanced around and didn't see anything he could use to snag the keys out of Mr. Jaggerman's hand. There was a motion near Tintin's feet. He looked and saw Snowy, who wagged his tail apologetically. Tintin glared at him but then thought about it and realized that Snowy might be better able to get to Mr. Jaggerman's bunk than Tintin himself.

He climbed part of the way up the rack of bunks, keeping his toes on the edge of the bottom one and reaching up to

hold on to the frame of the third. Snowy got the idea immediately. He skipped right up to the top bunk just as Tintin
stretched out and Mr. Jaggerman shifted in his sleep. Tintin's fingertips brushed against the keys. One more stretch
and he would have them!

Then the entire ship rolled again, more violently than
before, and the whole rack of bunks broke away from the
wall, with Tintin clinging to it and Snowy standing on
Mr. Jaggerman's bunk suddenly digging into the covers. He
came up with a sandwich in his jaws. "Not the sandwich!"
Tintin whispered. "The keys!"

He shoved Snowy across the bunk toward Mr. Jaggerman's flailing arm. The sailor hadn't awakened, but even
asleep he was responding to the motion of the bunk and the
ship.

Then the rack of bunks collided with the next. Both toppled, taking a third and fourth with them. An avalanche of
sleeping sailors buried Tintin, followed by whatever had
been in their bunks with them: empty bottles, lost shoes,
various guns and knives, a number of fish, and a single large
shark that had apparently had its own bunk. All of this collapsed onto the floor of the sleeping quarters as Haddock
watched.

Snowy ended up on top of the pile. He had lost the sandwich and was sniffing at the shark. Tintin's fist, holding the keys, burst through the pile, and he slowly worked himself free. He shot Haddock a glance. Apparently there had been no need for all the sneaking around; these men would not have awakened if lightning had struck inside the room.

Haddock clapped, slowly and quietly, as Tintin made his way across the landscape of sprawled sailors. Outside, he took the keys from Tintin and said, "You're a brave lad. My heart was in my mouth, I don't mind telling you."

They hurried through the ship back to the locked door. "Well, something was in my mouth, anyway," Haddock went on. "My stomach's been a bit unsettled lately...." He went through the keys and selected one.

"Hurry up, Captain," Tintin said. He was still tense from his misadventures in the bunk room. "We've no time to lose."

Then, as Haddock opened the door, Tintin saw what was inside. It wasn't a way out. It wasn't a way anywhere. It was a storeroom, and Haddock went rooting through the shelves, stuffing his pockets with all the bottles he could carry. "Bingo!" he said. "Just the necessities, of course."

Tintin stood aghast. All of this, for bottles of whiskey?

What about the mutiny? What about Sakharine? What about the secret of the *Unicorn*? Tintin was starting to think that he might have made better progress if he'd never met Captain Haddock. It was on the tip of his tongue to say so.

But then Captain Haddock looked at him, his pockets filled with little bottles, and Tintin couldn't say anything. Suddenly the captain looked like a man filled with purpose. He shot Tintin a wink. "To the lifeboats!" he said.

By the time they got to the hatch that led out onto the deck, Captain Haddock was halfway through one of the bottles he had liberated from the storeroom. He was muttering something about needing to calm his stomach in such stormy seas. Tintin just hoped he would remember where the lifeboats were.

They paused by the hatch to listen. Occasionally Tintin saw a sweep of light around the edges of the hatch. He thought he also heard voices. Putting two and two together, he figured out that the *Karaboudjan*'s crew — those who weren't sleeping in a pile below deck — were still looking for him and Captain Haddock. It was going to be a tricky trek to the lifeboats.

Captain Haddock apparently felt differently. "Let's go, lad," he said, and flung the hatch open, plunging out onto the deck...and almost running straight into a sailor, who happened to be passing by on a search sweep. Tintin pulled Captain Haddock back as the sailor made a grab for him. Taking the bottle from Captain Haddock's hand, Tintin cocked his arm to knock the man out with it.

As he swung, the bottle disappeared. Tintin's momentum carried him forward, though, and just as the hapless sailor figured out what was happening, Tintin knocked him out cold with a single punch.

Shaking his sore hand, Tintin glared at Haddock. "My stomach," Haddock said, and took a drink. Then he pointed across the deck. "There are the lifeboats!"

The *Karaboudjan* rocked on the stormy sea as Tintin, Snowy, and Haddock made their way toward the lifeboats, unhooked one, and started to shove it toward the edge of the deck. Held in place by a rope sling, it teetered at the edge of a gap in the deck railing above the churning water. The ropes went up over a gantry like a small crane and were wound around the gantry frame. A single person could unwind them and hang on to them while getting into the boat. Then, when the ropes were released, the boat would fall away from the *Karaboudjan*. Tintin looked at the sea and was suddenly uncertain about whether jumping into a lifeboat was the best course of action. A wave crest crashed around the *Karaboudjan*'s bow, wetting all three of them.

Captain Haddock unwound the ropes and braced one foot on the lifeboat's gunwale. He looked as if he was ready to cast off and jump right then, but he was distracted at that moment by a door that opened nearby, spilling light out onto the deck along with the unmistakable beeping of Morse code. Tintin and Haddock ducked behind the lifeboat, uncomfortably close to the edge of the deck and the frothing sea below, as Allan and Tom went through the door and shut it behind them. "It's Allan!" Haddock said in a quiet fury. "Traitor! Mutineer!"

"Is that the bridge?" Tintin asked.

"Aye," Haddock growled. "On the other side of the radio room."

Radio room, Tintin thought. He had an idea. "Wait here, Captain," he said. "Sound the alarm if anyone comes."

Haddock looked relieved that Tintin didn't want him to go along. "Careful, Tintin!" he warned, lifting a bottle to his lips.

Tintin and Snowy crossed the deck toward the steps that

led up to the radio-room door where Allan and Tom had entered. He heard a sailor complaining somewhere on the deck. "There's no one here!" the sailor grumbled, sweeping his flashlight lazily across the lifeboat and completely failing to notice that the ropes were all undone. "Who are we looking for, anyway?"

The sailor passed around the bridge, still complaining, and Tintin risked a glance through the window next to the door. Allan and Tom were huddled over a transmitter inside. Tintin could just make out what they were saying.

"Message just come through, boss," Tom said. "The Milanese Nightingale has landed. Waiting in the wings for action."

Milanese Nightingale, Tintin thought. It must be a code name. What could it mean? A mystery within a mystery.

He looked in again as Allan plucked the message from Tom's hand. "Maybe this'll cheer him up," Allan said as he and Tom left the radio room through an interior door. Tintin figured they were going to report to Sakharine.

After they left, he and Snowy sneaked into the radio room. Snowy immediately spotted a plate of sandwiches on a table next to a coffeepot. He jumped up onto the table and dug in as Tintin rummaged through the radio desk.

He looked at charts, flipped through pads filled with scribbled notations and Morse code notes...and stopped when he came across a brochure. BAGGHAR, it said, over a picture of a sunlit seaside city. Behind it, mountains rose around a gleaming white palace built at the base of a dam. Beyond the dam was a shimmering expanse of water, surprising in the midst of the dry country that surrounded it. A portrait of a smiling, bearded man was inset over part of the water. Tintin read the brochure quickly: *The Sultanate of Bagghar*...

He turned the page....*Ruled over by Sheik Omar Ben Salaad, whose love of music and culture is matched only by his love of*...

He turned another page and couldn't believe what he saw. "Great snakes, Snowy!" he said. He stuck the brochure in his pocket and looked again at a chart tacked to the wall next to the radio desk. *Bagghar*...

Tintin had an idea. He went to the transmitter, found the frequency he needed, and started tapping out a message. Good thing he knew Morse code, he thought. There was no time to waste, and only one way he could think of to get help.

CHAPTER 9

Out on the deck, Captain Haddock had finished his bottle and decided it was time to make the final preparations for their departure by lifeboat. He shoved the boat through the gap in the railing and out over the water. It rocked back and forth, hanging by some ropes slung over pulleys built on the side of the *Karaboudjan*'s deck. Captain Haddock held on to the other ends of those ropes, waiting for Tintin and the dog to come back so they could get going. His hand was getting cramped from gripping the ropes.

"Tintin!" he called out, throwing the empty bottle into

the boat. It landed with a clonk. What was the lad up to in there?

Someone sat up in the boat, nearly giving Captain Haddock a heart attack. It was a sailor, rubbing his head. Captain Haddock realized he must have hit him in the head with his discarded bottle. *Barnacles*, he thought. Just his luck.

Seeing the captain, the sailor drew a pistol from his belt and said, "Hey! Put your hands up!"

Captain Haddock had never been the kind of person to argue with someone who was pointing a gun at him. Not even a scurvy mutineer. He put his hands up, letting go of the ropes in the process. The ropes whipped against the bottom of the boat and snapped around the sailor's legs as the boat fell out from underneath him, splashing into the waves. The sailor flipped upside down and dropped until the ropes tangled in the pulleys, bringing him just a few feet above the water. He lost his gun as he grabbed for the ropes.

"Let that be a lesson to you!" Captain Haddock shouted down at him.

He looked around the deck. The search parties appeared to have moved on. He sighed and began to untie the next lifeboat.

Tintin had almost finished sending his message when the inside door to the radio room burst open and Tom spotted him. "In here! He's in here!" Tom shouted. Tintin could see Allan rushing up behind Tom.

Tom leveled his gun at Tintin, but Snowy leaped from the table, trailing bits of uneaten sandwich behind him, and sank his teeth into Tom's arm. The gun went off, and the bullet broke the window. Jumping up from the transmitter, Tintin socked Tom twice in the jaw, the combination knocking the thug backward into Allan. In the confusion, Tintin grabbed Tom's gun and ran out onto the deck.

He took the stairs in a single bound and skidded to a halt when he saw that the lifeboat was gone!

"Snowy!" he said. "Captain Haddock has—"

Snowy took off down the deck toward the stern. "Wait!" Tintin commanded. Then he saw what Snowy had seen. Captain Haddock had for some reason moved on to another lifeboat. What was he doing? Had he dropped the first one? Tintin ran after Snowy, hoping to get to Captain Haddock before he dropped this boat, too. They might not get a chance at a third.

"Captain, get ready!" Tintin called out. "Here we come!"

Allan was shouting from the radio-room door. Other sailors had appeared on the upper decks of the *Karaboudjan's* bridge. "Get him!" Allan shouted. Then he started shooting!

Captain Haddock looked up as he heard the commotion, and the lifeboat ropes slipped from his hands. The boat slipped and dangled at an angle from the pulleys. Haddock flinched away from a ricocheting bullet and fell into the boat, landing next to Snowy, who had just jumped in. There was a crash of breaking glass. Tintin dove headlong after Snowy and the captain as bullets whined through the air all around. He landed in the bottom of the boat. "Let go, Captain!"

"I can't!" Captain Haddock yelled. "I already did!"

Tintin looked up and grabbed on to one of the oarlocks as the boat swung and banged into the *Karaboudjan's* hull. The last rope had slipped off the pulley and jammed. It was looped around the lifeboat's bow, caught fast on an oarlock on one side and the boat on the other. There was no way to pull it off without lifting the boat, which was far too heavy to lift even if Tintin could have gotten back up on deck to do it. They were sitting ducks. Bullets from the *Karaboudjan*'s crew were coming closer.

A spotlight from the main deck targeted them. Now Tintin, Captain Haddock, and Snowy were in real trouble. The crew's bullets wouldn't miss them for much longer.

Tintin didn't like guns very much, but as the spotlight shone down on them from the bridge, he found a use for one. He aimed carefully with the pistol he had swiped and shot out the spotlight, plunging them back into darkness. The lifeboat swung, and he tugged vainly on the rope to free the boat, knowing it wouldn't work but not sure what else to do.

The rope wouldn't budge. Right at the railing, not twenty feet from Tintin, a sailor took up a firing stance. "I've got you now!" he shouted. The sailor took careful aim, but the *Karaboudjan* rolled in the sea and he had to readjust.

That bought Tintin a critical moment. *One shot*, Tintin thought. *That's all I'm going to get.*

He, too, took careful aim...and shot through the last rope holding up the lifeboat!

The boat fell into the ocean with a huge splash, soaking everyone on board. Tintin spluttered and threw Tom's gun overboard, grabbing an oar. Haddock already had the other one in hand, and they rowed for their lives as bullets smacked into the water. At the railing, the sailor was cursing. Another searchlight came on and swept the nearby waters. The glare nearly blinded Tintin, but he could just make out the figure of Sakharine emerging from the radio room onto the deck. He also spotted the other lifeboat that was bobbing in the ocean with the unlucky sailor whom Haddock had dropped overboard. He had finally untangled himself from the rope and was now adrift.

An idea came to Tintin. He pulled in his oar and flattened himself in the bottom of the boat. "Captain! Get down!" he said.

Captain Haddock got the idea. So did Snowy. All three of them hid from the searchlight. A signal flare blazed into life over the water, and Tintin heard a sailor call out, "There he is!"

But the searchlight was not on them. *This just might work,* Tintin thought. He dared a glimpse over the lifeboat's gunwale as the hulk of the *Karaboudjan* swung slowly around and bore down on the other lifeboat. "Full speed!" someone on the ship sang out. It sounded like Tom. A moment later the lifeboat was smashed to splinters by the *Karaboudjan's* bow.

The boat occupied by Tintin, Captain Haddock, and

Snowy drifted farther away. The seas were starting to calm a little, but waves still slapped over the lifeboat's gunwales. Captain Haddock bailed out water with his hat as the *Karaboudjan* corrected its course, aiming for Bagghar once more. They watched the spotlight from the *Karaboudjan* pick out the wreckage of the other lifeboat, waiting for the inevitable moment when Sakharine figured out what had happened and turned the *Karaboudjan* to look for them.

But a minute passed, and then another, and still the *Karaboudjan* steamed on. The searchlight played back and forth over the wreckage and then winked out.

"I think we can row now, Captain," Tintin said.

"Then row we shall, Tintin," Captain Haddock said, and they put their backs into it.

Looking over the railing of the *Karaboudjan*, Sakharine thought he was going to explode. "You idiots!" he raged. "What have you done?"

Next to him, Tom gazed down at the wreckage with pride. An empty whiskey bottle floated amid the pieces of the lifeboat, a sure sign that Captain Haddock had been there. "We killed them, boss," he said with great satisfaction. "Just like you wanted."

Sakharine grabbed Tom and forced him up against the railing, bending him over backward. Tom's eyes popped. "No," Sakharine said. "Not like I wanted. I needed Haddock alive!"

He was about to throw Tom overboard, just to make himself feel better, when Allan said, "Wait a minute, boss. There are two boats missing!"

"What?" Sakharine said. He looked down the railing and saw that Allan, for once, was right. There was a second boat gone.

"So that one must have been a decoy!" Tom said.

Sakharine flung Tom away from him. Tom's shoes scraped the deck as he tried to keep his balance. He fell into a sitting position, and Sakharine noticed something near Tom's right foot. A piece of paper.

He bent to pick it up. On it was written the word *Bagghar*, and below that a string of dots and dashes.

Ah, he thought, looking out over the dark water. *Tintin, you are perhaps a bit more clever than I'd thought.*

"They're on to us and our destination," Sakharine said, holding up the piece of paper so that all his imbecile henchmen could see it. "Find them! Make absolutely certain they never reach Bagghar!"

Leaving them to make preparations, he stalked to the stern of the *Karaboudjan*, where a seaplane, standing by on a catapult launcher, waited. Tintin and Haddock might think they had escaped him, but they were about to find out that a head start on a rowboat wasn't worth much when your adversary could fly.

CHAPTER 10

The sun rose over a seemingly endless ocean. Haddock was leaning against one gunwale, Snowy was looking out over the other, and Tintin was rowing hard by himself. "We have to get to Bagghar ahead of Sakharine," he said.

"I know! I know!" Haddock said. Then, after a brief pause, he added, "Why?"

Tintin tried not to be annoyed. "Because Ben Salaad has got the third model ship."

"How do you know?" Haddock asked. He sat up straighter and seemed to focus, at least for the moment. "Who's Ben Salaad?"

Tintin shipped the oars and dug the brochure from the radio room out of his pocket. He showed Haddock the picture from its interior page. "The sheik of Bagghar. He collects old ships for display in his palace. This is the prize of his collection."

Haddock looked at the picture showing a glossy full-page photograph of the *Unicorn* in an ornate case, behind thick glass. "Blistering blue barnacles! That *is* the *Unicorn*!" Haddock cried.

"Captain, do you see this distortion around the model?" Tintin pointed to the slight waviness of parts of the model ship in the picture. "It means Ben Salaad exhibits it behind bulletproof glass."

"And Sakharine is going there to steal it!" Haddock said, finally getting the picture.

"He has a secret weapon: the Milanese Nightingale," Tintin said, even though he didn't know what kind of weapon the Milanese Nightingale was. He had the faintest beginning of an idea but not enough to be certain of anything. "But that won't be enough to solve the mystery, and that is why Sakharine needs you. That's why he took you prisoner! There is something he needs you to remember."

"I don't follow you," Haddock said. Tintin could see his fingers starting to search his pockets for a bottle.

"I read it in a book. Only a true Haddock can discover the secret of the *Unicorn*." Tintin looked at Haddock, and Haddock looked at Tintin. *Come on, Captain*, Tintin thought. Snowy whined and nudged Haddock's knee.

"I don't remember anything about anything," Haddock said eventually.

"But you must know about your ancestor Sir Francis!" Tintin said. "It's your family legacy!"

Haddock was now definitely patting his pockets. "My memory isn't what it used to be."

"What did it used to be?" Tintin asked.

"I've forgotten."

Frustrated, Tintin was silent for a while. He was trying to work things out in his head, but he was also imagining how great the story would be when he finally got it. The secret of the *Unicorn*! What he needed at the moment was to motivate Captain Haddock, break him out of his self-pity—remind him what he was good at.

But what was he good at? As far as Tintin could tell, Captain Haddock was so far gone into his bottle that he had lost his ship, his family history...everything.

What did a man like that have left?

Tintin wasn't sure, but he knew he'd have to figure it out or else Sakharine would get the third *Unicorn* and they would never solve the mystery. Tintin refused to let that happen; he had his teeth into this mystery now, and he would not let it go. He would row to Bagghar himself if he had to . . . if he only knew which way to row.

Aha, he thought. *Captain Haddock may be full of self-pity, and he may be a little too fond of liquor, but he is still a seaman.*

"Captain," Tintin said, "can you get us to Bagghar?"

He deliberately asked the question in a tone of voice that made it clear that he didn't think Captain Haddock could do it. Reverse psychology!

And it worked. "What sort of a stupid question is that?" Haddock exploded. "Give me those oars. I'll show you some real seamanship, laddie."

He moved toward Tintin and picked up the oars, flipping them over his shoulder as he kept shouting. "I'll not be doubted by some pipsqueak tuft of ginger and his irritating dog. I am master and commander of the seas!"

This is working perfectly, Tintin thought. Then Haddock pivoted on his heel, heading back to his end of the boat, and as he turned, the oars over his shoulder swept around and knocked both Tintin and Snowy out cold. They slumped in their seats and Haddock kept up his rant. "I know these waters better than the warts on me mother's face! Every wave of them is like a compass needle. The secrets of the deeps are mine and mine alone!"

He planted himself on one of the rowing benches and slapped the oars into the other set of oarlocks. "Look at the pair of them, fast asleep!" Haddock said. "Typical land-lubbers. No stamina these days. Never mind, I'll get ye there, Tintin."

It felt good to row, thought Captain Haddock as he dug the oars into the water. They would be in Bagghar in no time, and then they would see about that third model *Unicorn* and this Sheik Whatshisname. Tintin would see that Captain Archibald Haddock was not a man to trifle with.

Back home, Thompson and Thomson rarely had a day that they looked forward to as much as this one. Usually they had to chase criminals, but today's agenda contained a much more pleasant task. They walked together along the streets near the Old Street Market, scanning the crowd. "He does frequent this area, does he not?" Thomson said.

Thompson nodded. "If our pickpocket does, he must as well, isn't that right? Ah, there he is."

As Thompson pointed, Thomson also saw the gray-haired, gloved man strolling down the street. And as they saw him, he saw them. "Oh my!" he said.

"Mr. Silk?" Thompson asked.

"Yes," Silk said. He looked nervous.

Perfectly understandable, given the circumstances, Thompson thought. "My name is Thompson."

"And Thomson," Thomson said, tipping his hat.

"We're police officers," they said in unison.

Silk's reaction surprised them. "Oh, crumbs!" he said, and turned away, knocking over an old woman who happened to be coming out of a nearby pet shop with a cage full of canaries. The cage broke open as Silk stumbled to the sidewalk, and the canaries fluttered around his head, chirping at their unexpected freedom.

"Mr. Silk!" Thompson said. "Are you all right?"

The owner of the pet shop ran out with a net and began catching the canaries as a passerby helped the old woman to her feet. Seeing that this situation was under control, the two Interpol detectives concentrated on Silk. "Are you all right, sir?" Thomson asked.

"No need to run away, sir." Thompson dusted Silk off.

Thomson joined in, straightening Silk's tie. "No, no. You see, yesterday, we very nearly caught the pickpocket who's been terrorizing the town."

"Pickpocket," Silk said.

"We pulled his jacket off," Thompson went on, "and inside we found a wallet. A wallet with your name and address."

He held it up, and Silk said, "That's my wallet."

"It's obviously stolen from you," Thompson said.

"No, no!" Silk cried out, most unexpectedly. "That's my wallet!"

Thompson and Thomson exchanged a glance. "Are you all right, sir?" Thomson asked.

"We didn't mean to startle you," Thompson said. "Let us help you to your apartment."

Silk's apartment was just a short distance down the street; Thompson and Thomson knew this from the address in his wallet. They led him there and stopped at the door, where Silk nodded to them. "Thank you so much. No need to come in," he said, and coughed nervously. "I'll be quite all right, really."

"No, but we insist!" Thomson said. He and Thompson shared a sense of responsibility to the citizens of the city. They could not leave an obviously shaken man of Silk's age by himself, not until they were sure he would be all right. Passing pedestrians looked at them, wondering if they were witnessing an arrest. It would be the most exciting thing most of them had seen in ages.

Thompson did not want to make a scene. The old man was clearly in distress. He waved the gawkers back. "About your business!" he said. "This is a police matter."

"No need whatsoever," Silk was saying. "Really, no need..."

"Better safe than sorry," Thompson said. He raised his voice and called out so that everyone could hear. "It's the least we can do!"

With great relief at being away from the eyes of the crowd, he and Thomson led Silk into his apartment and sat him down in an armchair. "There we are."

"Oh," Silk said. "Thank you."

Thompson and Thomson patted Silk on the shoulder and took a look around the apartment, admiring its neatness and the way that all the wallets on the large bookshelf in the middle of the room were labeled and organized.

Wait... the wallets?!

The detectives looked at each other, stunned. "Good grief," Thompson said. "What's all this?"

Silk slumped forward in his chair. "It's my . . . collection."

"What a lot of wallets," Thomson observed.

Straightening up again, Silk said, "I can't help it. It started with coin purses . . . and sort of . . . went on from there, really."

It is amazing what people would do, Thompson thought. "You want to be careful," he admonished Silk. "Haven't you heard there's a pickpocket about?"

Nodding, Thomson chimed in, "Yes, he'd love this. Can you imagine?"

The two detectives were not very good at detecting what was right in front of them — but Silk didn't know that.

Silk appeared to be offended, though neither of the detectives could understand why. "What do you mean, pickpocket?" he said coldly.

"A master criminal," Thompson said. "A bag-snatching, purse-pilfering, wallet-lifting sneak thief."

To their disbelief, Silk now seemed to be on the verge of tears. "I'm not a bad person," he said, his voice quavering in time with the tremble of his lower lip. "I'm a . . . kleptomaniac."

"A what?" Thompson asked.

Thomson leaned over and whispered in his ear. "It's a fear of open spaces."

Ah, Thompson thought. It was hard to keep track of all the medical terms these days. "Poor man," he whispered back. "No wonder he keeps his wallets in the living room."

During their brief consultation, Silk's mood shifted radically yet again. "Wallets!" he said with joy. "I just can't resist the lovely little things. It's a...it's a harmless little habit, really."

Thompson's interest was piqued by the rows and rows of wallets. He pulled one from the shelf with his finger as he would have drawn a book from a bookshelf.

What he saw astonished him. "Good heavens," he said. "Thomson, look at this! His name's Thompson, too!"

Thomson's eyebrows shot up. "Oh, what a coincidence!" He took a different wallet from the shelf, looked at it, and said, "No, Thompson, this is *Thomson* without a *p*—as in 'psychic.' "

"No, no, no. It's *Thompson* with a *p*," Thompson said. "As in 'psychologist.' "

"Look at this one," Silk said, but neither detective paid attention. "A green one that I managed to pick from a pickpocket actually pickpocketing at the time. And this one..."

He went on as the detectives grew more and more annoyed with each other. "How dare you, sir?" Thomson was saying, and Thompson answered right back. "How dare *you*, sir?"

"Good heavens, Thompson, you've got it all wrong!" They began brandishing wallets at each other as Silk looked back and forth from one of them to the next.

"No, you have it all wrong, and there is a *p* in 'psychic'!" Thompson exclaimed.

"I'm not your sidekick," Thomson said in a huff, mishearing him. "You are mine!"

"Smell it, won't you?" Silk said, pressing a wallet to his face. "Piggy leather. Oh, I love piggy leather." He was crumbling under the pressure and starting to get delirious.

"How dare you?" Thompson said in great high dudgeon. "I met you first."

"No, you didn't."

"Yes, I did."

"No, you did not," Thomson insisted.

"Yes, I did."

"Didn't!"

"Did!"

"Didn't!"

All the while they were dimly conscious that poor Mr. Silk was talking to them, but it was vitally important to both Thompson and Thomson that this business of seniority and who was sidekick to whom be sorted out immediately. So neither of them heard Silk cry out, "Listen! I can't stand it anymore! All right, I'll come quietly!"

He began to shove wallets into the detectives' hands, tears in his eyes, saying, "Take them, take them!"

Thomson recoiled. "What are you doing?"

"Take them all!" Silk shouted.

"Stop this at once, sir!" Thomson said.

Thompson caught Silk by the shoulder. "Pull yourself together, man! We can't take your wallets. Do we look like thieves?"

"Good heavens, Thompson!" Thomson said then. Thompson looked away from Silk to see that Thomson was opening yet another wallet. "This looks familiar," Thomson went on. "It can't be...?"

Then both of them saw the name and address. "It is!" Thompson exclaimed.

"Tintin!" both of them said together.

CHAPTER 11

Tintin was dozing peacefully in the boat until Snowy's barking roused him. He yawned and stretched and opened his eyes...to see Captain Haddock warming his hands over a blazing fire...right in the middle of the boat!

"Captain!" Tintin said, sitting bolt upright and scooting back from the fire. "What have you done?"

"No need to thank me," Captain Haddock said. "You looked a little cold, so I lit a wee fire." He took a swig from a half-empty bottle that must have survived his fall into the lifeboat from the *Karaboudjan*.

"In a boat!?" Tintin looked around and then back at the fire, suddenly noticing what Captain Haddock had used for wood. "Those are the oars! We need those oars!"

"Yes, yes," said Captain Haddock. "But not for much longer! Can't you see the boat's on fire?"

Tintin leaned over the gunwale and scooped water in his hands, sloshing it into the bottom of the boat. The fire hissed and spat. "Have you gone mad?" he said. "Quick, Captain. Help me! Help me quick!"

Captain Haddock looked shocked at Tintin's response, as if only then did he realize the consequences of his own action. "He's right!" the old sailor said, clapping one hand over his face and raising the other to the skies. "What have I done?"

With that he upended the liquor bottle over the fire. "No, Captain! Not that!" Tintin cried out, but it was too late. The fire roared up in a great orange mushroom, the heat of it singeing Captain Haddock's beard, Tintin's hair, and even Snowy's whiskers. All three of them jumped overboard at once.

Tintin flailed his way back to the surface. Snowy paddled in circles around him, sneezing seawater. Around the stern of the lifeboat, Tintin could see Captain Haddock trying to swim with one arm and keep his precious bottle out of the water at the same time. On the boat, the fire burned merrily. There was only one thing to do. Tintin caught hold of the boat's gunwale and hoisted himself up, pushing down to tip the boat. For a moment, he was balanced perfectly on the gunwale. "Tintin!" Captain Haddock cried. "Don't get in the boat. It's on fire, lad!"

Tintin thought of a great many things he might say, but he didn't say any of them. He dropped back into the water and pulled down on the side of the boat with both hands, tipping it up. It hung on edge, and Tintin pulled harder. He was underwater again, and over his head he heard the rush and gurgle of water pouring into the boat. He got his feet behind him and gave the barely submerged side of the boat a push.

The boat capsized, with Tintin underneath it. He looked up through stinging salt water and saw the fire wink out, doused by the water and smothered from the lack of air at the same time. He kicked out from under the boat and resurfaced at its side, clinging to it by the ridge of its upturned keel. Smoke rose from charred wood and the few remaining embers where the fire had burned completely through the hull.

"Well, this is a fine mess," Tintin said. Snowy paddled over to him and rested his paws in the crook of Tintin's arm.

Captain Haddock caught hold of the boat and shook his head sadly. "I'm weak," he said.

"We're stranded here," Tintin said.

"Selfish," Captain Haddock said.

"With no hope of rescue," Tintin added.

"Hopeless!" Captain Haddock cried miserably.

"While Sakharine and his men are halfway to Bagghar," Tintin went on, venting the last of his frustration.

"Poor, miserable wretch!" Captain Haddock said.

Tintin splashed water over the embers. "Yes, all right," he said over the hiss. "That's enough of that." He couldn't stand it when people wallowed in their own mistakes.

"It was his fault, you see," Haddock said. "It was Sir Francis!"

"How do you work that one out?" Tintin asked. He was skeptical, and he could see that Snowy was, too. It was a cheeky move to blame your personal failings on an ancestor who died more than three centuries in the past.

Haddock held up his bottle, saw that it was empty, and slumped against the overturned lifeboat. "Because he was a man of great courage and bold exploits!" he exclaimed. "No one like him has ever existed in my family since!" He brandished the bottle. "I know I'll never be like him!" Haddock banged his head against the boat. "No, it's far better that I end it now. Put us both out of our misery."

For his part, Tintin didn't want to be put out of his misery. In fact, he wasn't miserable. Snowy seemed to be, though. He was whining against Tintin's shirtfront. Then he barked.

"What is it, Snowy?" Tintin asked. Snowy wasn't usually the kind of dog who complained for no reason...unlike certain sea captains Tintin knew. Usually if he interrupted a conversation, it was because he had something important to say.

"I'm going to lower myself into the sea," Haddock said theatrically. "Into the cold embrace of the big blue..."

Tintin looked up into the sky, rolling his eyes...and saw a seaplane! A rush of excitement ran through him, and then a pang of suspicion. "Those are Portuguese markings," he said as the plane banked in their direction. It was bright yellow, with stubby wings and CN-3411 stenciled boldly across both sides of its fuselage. "Where is the *Karaboudjan* registered?"

Haddock seemed relieved that Tintin had changed the subject from Haddock's failures and misery. He looked up

121

and saw the plane, and then—with an agility Tintin would not have believed had he not seen it himself—jumped up on the overturned lifeboat and began waving. "We're saved! We're saved! It's a sign from above!"

The seaplane's engine revved up as it accelerated into a low approach. It wasn't landing, Tintin thought. It was going much too fast for that…and then he saw flashes from one of its wings. A split second later, bullets slammed into the boat and churned up the waters around them as the sound of machine-gun fire battered their ears!

Tintin ducked behind the boat, Snowy hanging on to his sleeve. Captain Haddock, in a fury, shook his fists at the seaplane, which was banking around for another pass. "Troglodytes!"

"Captain, get down!" Tintin yelled.

"Mutant malingerers!" Haddock screamed. "Freshwater politicians!"

Something bumped into Tintin. A case. He thought he recognized it as something that was part of every lifeboat's emergency supplies. Sure enough, when he opened it, he saw a flare gun inside, packed in foam, which had kept the case afloat. "Bad news, Captain!" he cried out. "This flare gun only has one flare!"

Haddock broke off his rant at the seaplane, which was nearly within firing range again. "What's the good news?" he called out.

"We've got one flare," Tintin said. He loaded the gun and flattened himself against the curve of the lifeboat's hull, waiting for his chance.

Again, gunfire erupted. The seaplane's second volley hit the lifeboat, reducing it to splinters. Captain Haddock tumbled off into the water, grasping at a piece of the boat to stay above the surface. Tintin braced both of his hands around the flare gun's grip, resting them on the remains of the keel. Bullets zinged and whined around him, smacking into the water.

He aimed and fired with a *boomph!* The seaplane roared directly overhead, so low that Captain Haddock and Tintin both reflexively ducked under the water. When they surfaced again, Snowy was barking and Tintin saw a thick trail of black smoke coming from the seaplane's engine. *Amazing*, he thought.

"Tintin, you got him!" Captain Haddock cheered. "Right in the blockhole! Well done, my boy."

The plane's engine sputtered out as it was in the middle of coming around for what surely would have been a last pass at Tintin and Captain Haddock. It landed in the water in a great wave of spray, then sat rocking on the waves. One of the pilots got out, stood on the pontoon, and worked his way to the front of the fuselage, popping open the cowling over the engine. A cloud of black smoke enveloped him.

Tintin and Captain Haddock, with Snowy between them, huddled against the remains of the lifeboat, kicking their feet to propel it a little closer to the seaplane. The pilot's voice floated over the water, but they couldn't understand what he was saying.

"Stay here, Captain," Tintin said.

He dove under the water as Captain Haddock said something—he wasn't sure what. For as long as he could hold his breath, he kicked along until he came to the rear of one of the seaplane's floats. He surfaced and quietly gulped in air. "Don't take your eyes off of them!" the pilot at the cowling was saying.

A second pilot, inside the cockpit, said, "Hurry up!"

The first pilot had waved away most of the smoke. "Just as I thought," he grumbled. "The ignition lead's been cut. Lucky shot."

Tintin swam along under the plane as silently as he could.

"One more pass and we'll finish them off," the pilot inside the cockpit was saying.

Here we go, Tintin thought. He could not let the two pilots get the seaplane back in the air . . . and if it was just an ignition lead, they would have it fixed in no time.

On the other hand, if he could get control of the plane, he could fix the ignition lead himself. . . .

Fortune favors the bold, Tintin told himself. He vaulted up onto the pontoon, the plane rocking with his weight and throwing the pilots off balance. Tintin leveled the flare gun at them and said, "Put your hands in the air!"

They stared at him, amazed. Before either of them had time to get a good look at the gun and figure out that it wouldn't actually fire bullets, Tintin jammed it into the first pilot's side. "*Now!*" he yelled.

The pilot's hands shot into the air. Out of the corner of his eye, Tintin saw that the second pilot inside the cockpit had done the same. Just then, the remains of the lifeboat gently bumped into the pontoon. Snowy scrabbled up onto the plane, and a moment later came Captain Haddock. "Good work, lad," he said. "Now all we have to do is fly to Bagghar!"

CHAPTER 12

Five minutes later, the pilots were tied up in the back
of the plane and Tintin was puzzling over the flight
manual. Captain Haddock peered over his shoulder while
Snowy growled at the pilots. "You, ah, you *do* know what
you're doing?" Captain Haddock inquired hopefully. "Eh,
Tintin?"

"Um," Tintin said. "More or less."

He had repaired the ignition lead himself. A wire was a
wire; it was easy to fix. Flying a plane, however...

"Well, which is it?" Haddock pressed. "More or less?"

Tintin flipped a switch, and the plane's propeller began to turn as the engine rumbled to life. "Relax," Tintin said. "I interviewed a pilot once."

Captain Haddock looked a little green around the gills. Tintin got the plane moving, looking from the instrument panel to the manual and back. From the rear of the plane, he heard one of the pilots say, "Oh, no."

"Never fear," Tintin said. He pulled the control stick back, and the seaplane lifted off the ocean's surface, gaining altitude and arcing away from the drifting bits of the lifeboat, heading in the general direction that Tintin thought the plane had come from in the first place. Now they were back in the hunt! They would surely beat Sakharine to Bagghar by air!

"Which way to North Africa?" he called out over the sound of the engine and the air rushing past the open cockpit window. Snowy was hanging his head out, his ears flapping in the wind.

No one answered. The pilots were sulking in the back, and Captain Haddock was staring out the window. Tintin looked out to see what the captain was looking at. There was a speck on the water, far away, almost in the horizon. He banked toward it, keeping altitude for now. When they got a little closer, Tintin recognized the *Karaboudjan*!

"Captain, look!" he cried out. "We've caught up with them!"

Also, now they knew which way to go, since the *Karaboudjan* was steaming full speed for Bagghar. Tintin took a bearing and marked it on the compass set into the instrument panel. "North Africa, that way," he said.

"Wonderful," Captain Haddock said. Something about his tone of voice made Tintin look at him again as they passed over the big steel ship and then out over open ocean again. His eyes popped as he saw what the captain was seeing. "But do you think we might find another way?" Captain Haddock asked. "A way that doesn't take us through that wall of death there?"

A storm front like a solid black wall streaked with lightning loomed ahead of them. "We can't turn back!" Tintin said. "Not now."

From the back of the plane, he heard the pilots. "Oh, no," they were saying again.

"Don't worry," Tintin said. "Remember, you didn't think I could fly this thing, either."

Neither of them had anything to say to that.

The plane bucked when they hit the edge of the storm, bouncing Tintin in his seat. Haddock hit his head on the cockpit ceiling. The pilots in the back were thrown into each other. They started calling out advice to Tintin, in between cries of "Oh, no!"

Tintin kept control as lightning forked alarmingly close. The plane heaved and rolled through a cloud. A cabinet in the cockpit fell open and a bunch of bottles and little boxes fell out. Tintin glanced over and saw that Captain Haddock had seized one of the bottles. Its label read MEDICINAL SPIRITS. Tintin swatted the bottle out of the captain's hands. "No, Captain!" he said, trying to look in two directions at once. Snowy barked in alarm. "Those are for medicinal purposes only!"

"Quite right, laddie," Captain Haddock said. "Medicinal. Got it."

The storm was getting worse. Tintin couldn't believe it. As if a giant had caught it and thrown it like a paper airplane, the seaplane suddenly flipped into a barrel roll. Everyone banged and crashed in the cabin. Tintin righted the plane, but then it went into a steep dive. Tintin felt himself lifting away from the seat. He had a grip on the controls, which kept him anchored, but Captain Haddock floated up into the air. So did Snowy and the pilots. Somehow Captain Haddock had opened the bottle of medicinal spirits when Tintin wasn't looking, and the liquid floated around the cabin in globules.

Captain Haddock strained toward them, but just then, Tintin regained control of the plane and everyone crashed back to the floor...but then it went into another dive. The spirits spilled from the floating bottle as Captain Haddock cried out in dismay.

"No!" Tintin shouted. Captain Haddock looked at him guiltily. But Tintin didn't care about the spill. He was looking out the cockpit windows, watching as the plane's propeller was fluttering to a stop.

On the instrument panel, a red light flashed next to the fuel gauge.

"Fuel tank!" Tintin said. "It's almost empty. Captain, I've got a plan! The alcohol in that bottle might give us a few more miles. I need you to climb out onto the pontoons and pour it into the fuel tank."

Captain Haddock looked stricken. "Christopher Columbus!" he said.

He stood up and buckled on a parachute. One hand holding on to his hat, he opened the cabin door. Immediately his beard started blowing in the wind. At his feet, the two pilots lay quiet. They'd been knocked out by the plane's diving and bouncing. "There's a storm out there!" Captain Haddock said, as if Tintin hadn't noticed. "And lightning! And it's raining!"

"Do you call yourself a Haddock?" Tintin challenged him.

Captain Haddock glared at him. He stuck out his chin, drew himself up to his full height, took a step out the door... and disappeared.

"Captain!" Tintin yelled.

Nothing. Tintin called out again and again. Captain Haddock was gone! Tintin felt sudden crushing guilt. He should have known better than to send the captain out onto the wing of a plane! Captain Haddock wasn't bold and resourceful like his ancestors. Tintin had pushed him too hard, and now—

Captain Haddock's face appeared at Tintin's window!

"You're doing fine, Captain!" Tintin shouted through the glass. He was excited all over again, his guilt forgotten. It was working. Captain Haddock might yet prove worthy of his name! "Now pour the bottle into the tank. We're running on fumes!"

"Fumes!" Captain Haddock said, as if he had made a great discovery. Something hit Tintin's foot, and he looked down to see the bottle of medicinal spirits. It was empty!

He looked back outside to see that Captain Haddock had worked himself out onto the engine cowling. He opened the fuel cap, took a deep breath, and belched loudly into the tank. At the same time, Tintin flipped the ignition switch back and forth.

The propeller started to spin again as flames shot out from the engine compartment. "Captain, it's working!" Tintin yelled at the top of his lungs. He didn't know how, but Captain Haddock's breath was apparently so saturated with alcohol that the plane's engine could burn it!

At least for the moment. Captain Haddock sat up and blocked Tintin's view. Tintin started yelling that he couldn't see as Captain Haddock pointed ahead. "Land!" he sang out. "Land!"

Tintin shook his head. "We can't! We're not there yet!"

"No, *land*!"

A gigantic sand dune suddenly loomed into view through the part of the windshield Captain Haddock wasn't blocking. The captain was hollering, "Turn! Turn!" Tintin pulled on the controls, jerking the plane to one side and barely missing the dune.

"Starboard! Starboard!" Captain Haddock shouted.

Tintin steered the plane to the right. He heard noises

from behind him and looked back to see that the pilots had awakened and freed themselves. *Uh-oh*, he thought.

But the pilots were only concerned with saving themselves.

A flash of lightning blazed so close that Tintin could smell the ozone, and a loud thunderclap rang in his ears. Captain Haddock was catapulted off the plane's nose, and the pilots grabbed their parachutes and jumped out.

The plane hit the top of another sand dune and flames shot out of its engine again. It skipped across the sand before plowing across the crest of a third dune and skidding to a stop, tail in the air. The impact threw Tintin through the windshield and he hung forward, the propeller spinning inches from his face!

"Hang on, Tintin! I'm coming!" Captain Haddock said from a nearby pile of sand.

Snowy got hold of Tintin's pants and was trying to pull him to safety, but the boy was too big for the little terrier. The propeller zipped off some of Tintin's hair. Snowy was still tugging at him as Captain Haddock clambered up the dune and pulled Tintin off the side of the plane's nose. The propeller caught Captain Haddock's parachute and flung him violently to the ground, but the tangled parachute lines finally brought the propeller to a halt.

Tintin sat up and shook his head. The first things he saw were Snowy lying on his side, passed out from exertion, and the two pilots hanging by their parachutes from the rusted wreckage of a cargo ship. Everything was quiet. The storm was passing, and sunlight started to break through the clouds.

"Well," said Captain Haddock after a while. "What do we do now?"

Tintin didn't have a good answer, so he said what he always said in situations like this. "We go on," he said. "There's a mystery to solve!"

CHAPTER 13

Later that day, Tintin was wishing they were in the storm again. He was also regretting his decision to lead Captain Haddock and Snowy away from the wrecked plane. They had gone from an ocean of water to an ocean of sand. Tintin had the terrible feeling that he had led them on a charge to certain doom...but it was too late to go back.

They had been walking through the desert, the sun blazing down on them without mercy, for what seemed like years. "The land of thirst," Haddock was muttering over and over again. He had been for hours. "The land of thirst...The land of thirst!"

"Will you stop saying that?" Tintin snapped. The heat and his own thirst were making him a little impatient.

"You don't understand," Captain Haddock groaned. "I've run out. I've run out." He sank to his knees, and Tintin stopped to prevent him from falling face-first into the sand. "You don't know what that means," Captain Haddock said.

"Captain, we have to keep going," Tintin said. "One step at a time. Come on, on your feet." With Tintin's help, Haddock staggered back to his feet. "Lean your weight on me," Tintin said.

"A man can only hang on for so long without his vitals," Haddock gasped.

"Captain, calm down," Tintin said. "There are worse things than sobering up."

Haddock froze, and Tintin thought perhaps he had made the captain angry. But then he said, "Look, Tintin! We're saved!"

He shoved Tintin away and broke into a run across the sand, staring into the distance as Snowy bit down on Haddock's dangling suspenders to try to slow him down. The suspenders stretched and broke, snapping back into Snowy's face as Haddock ran faster, crying, "Water! Water!"

"Stop, Captain!" Tintin ran after him, with Snowy at his side. He couldn't see any water. "It's just a mirage!"

They caught up to Captain Haddock after a minute as the captain slowed to a dazed stagger and looked around in confusion. "But it was here," he said. "I saw it."

"It was just your mind playing tricks," Tintin said, trying to soothe him. "It's the heat."

Captain Haddock gazed sadly out over the rolling expanse of sand. A single tear rolled down his cheek, and he said quietly, "I have to go home."

"What?" Tintin didn't understand.

"I have to go back to the sea."

"Captain, you're hallucinating," Tintin said.

But as if Tintin had not spoken at all, Captain Haddock went on. He pointed toward a dune and said, "Look, did you ever see a more beautiful sight? She's turning into the wind, all sails set!" He had fallen in the middle of his misery, but now he got up again and described his vision. "Triple-masted, double decks, fifty guns…"

Tintin had been about to take drastic measures to snap Captain Haddock out of his hallucination, but this description stopped him dead. Was the captain seeing…? "The *Unicorn*?" Tintin said softly.

Nodding, Haddock said, "Isn't she a beauty?"

Could it be that the mirage would help Captain Haddock regain some of his lost memories and unravel part of the puzzle of the *Unicorn*? Even facing a blazing death in the middle of the desert, Tintin couldn't pass up the chance to find another clue. "Yes, yes, she is," he said, playing along to encourage Haddock to reveal more. "What else can you see?"

"She's got the wind behind her!" the captain said joyously. "Look at the pace she's setting! Barely a day out of Barbados, a hold full of rum and riches, and the hearts of the sailors set for home!"

"Yes," Tintin said. He could almost see it, the sand becoming ocean and the *Unicorn*, flying the king's ensign, surging into view, its sails billowing as it plowed through the high seas. The voice of a lookout called across the water, "Ship ahoy! Sail on the starboard bow!"

And Sir Francis Haddock, in the uniform of the royal navy, snapped his spyglass out to its full length, and through it saw the skull and crossbones unfurling from the other ship's mast. "It's the Jolly Roger!" the lookout shouted, but Sir Francis noticed something else: a red pennant flapping below the pirate flag.

In the desert, Captain Haddock turned to face Tintin,

saying, "The blood of every sea captain who looks upon that flag runs cold, for he knows he's facing a fight to the death. But Sir Francis is a Haddock, and Haddocks don't flee."

Then Captain Haddock peered through his empty bottle as if it were a spyglass, and Tintin was lost in the story once again.

"All hands on deck!" Sir Francis commanded. "Gunners to their stations. Let's unload the king's shot into these yellow-bellied, lily-livered sea slugs!" Turning to his first mate, he added, "Prepare to bring her about, Mr. Eckles!"

"Aye, aye, Captain!" Eckles said. "Prepare to bring her about!"

The pirate ship was close behind them as the *Unicorn* crested a wave and slowly heaved about in the trough between that wave and the next. Cannon fire exploded between the two ships. The *Unicorn*'s sails were shredded! The pirate ship closed the distance between them, and the heaving sea tilted the ships toward each other, tangling their masts and yardarms. They rode the waves together, both ships crashing and groaning in the waves. Smoke and fire blew across both decks, stinging the sailors' eyes.

"Mr. Eckles, secure the cargo!" Sir Francis bellowed. Then he issued a general order, his voice booming across the storm-tossed deck. "Prepare to repel boarders."

Twisting up, the pirate ship leaned over, its keel briefly scraping along the edge of the *Unicorn*'s deck. Pirates leaped across the gap as others swung from the pirate ship's deck into the *Unicorn*'s rigging. Still others landed on the upper decks. The shouts and cries of battle merged with the sounds of the storm and the groaning of ships' timbers. The two ships collided, and the pirate ship was badly damaged. It began to sink, and Sir Francis feared that it would drag the *Unicorn* down with it. He leaped into the rigging. A knife flew past his head, slitting the upturned brim of his hat and clipping away part of the red plume. But no knife was going to stop him from saving his ship! Up the mast he climbed.

When he reached the horizontal yardarm, he clamped his legs around the mast and began sawing at the tangled ropes that bound the two ships together. The *Unicorn* was listing as the pirate ship dragged at it. Sir Francis looked over and saw that the rear decks of the pirate ship were already underwater.

He shinnied out onto the yardarm and over to the mast of the pirate ship, closing in on the last rope holding the two ships together. Reaching the pirate ship's mast, he caught that rope and sawed through it with his cutlass. The loose end of the rope in his hand jerked him off the mast as the ships separated, and Sir Francis dangled free, one hand on the rope and the other brandishing his cutlass at the swarming deck below.

He swung back to the *Unicorn*'s mast and slid down to the deck, dispatching pirate after pirate. "Rally, ye sailors of the *Unicorn*!" he cried out. "Rally to the king and to Captain Haddock!"

His sailors answered with a cheer. On the deck, silhouetted by the smoke of muskets and a fire blazing somewhere on the rear decks, Sir Francis spotted the figure he'd been looking for. . . .

"And then he saw him," Captain Haddock whispered. His face was caked with sand, and his lips were parched and dry. "Rising from the dead!"

"Who?" Tintin asked.

But Haddock had fallen silent. He began to sweat as he struggled to hold on to the memory. "Captain!" Tintin said. "Captain, who did he see?"

The wind was the only sound for a minute or so. Then Captain Haddock said, "It's gone. . . ."

"What do you mean, gone?" Tintin protested. "What happened next?"

"By Jupiter, I have a beard," Captain Haddock said, fingering his chin. "Since when did I have a beard?"

"Captain, the *Unicorn*! Something happened on the *Unicorn*? It's the key to everything!" Tintin grabbed Captain Haddock and shook him a little. "You must try to remember!"

Haddock began to sway on his feet even after Tintin stopped shaking him. "The *Unicorn*?" he repeated. "What? I'm so terribly thirsty."

"Captain!" Tintin repeated in frustration. What could he do to get Haddock to remember?

"Tintin, what's happening to me?" Captain Haddock said fearfully. He sank to the ground, with Snowy pacing anxiously around him and Tintin supporting him.

Tintin knew exactly what was happening to Captain Haddock. Maybe none of them would ever get out of the desert, but at least one good thing came out of the experience. "And to think all it took was a day in the Sahara," he said when Captain Haddock was resting comfortably on the ground. "Congratulations, Captain. You're sober."

"Sober," Captain Haddock said as if he couldn't quite believe it. He mouthed the word several more times with a surprised smile on his cracked lips. Then he passed out, and Tintin was left to watch over him as the sun touched the horizon and the sand stretched endlessly in every direction.

Bagghar was far away. Sakharine was ahead of them in the race to capture the third model *Unicorn*....

One of these days, Tintin thought, *I'm going to tell this story to someone, and we will all laugh about it.*

But right then, things seemed pretty desperate.

CHAPTER 14

That night, a sandstorm struck without warning. Exhausted from the day under the desert sun and unable to move Captain Haddock, Tintin covered the unconscious captain as best he could and then hunkered down himself. At least sundown had brought cooler temperatures. Tintin had fallen asleep just at nightfall, but the storm woke him up. They were in a slight hollow behind a dune, with curtains of sand tearing through the air all around them. Tintin put Captain Haddock's hat over his mouth and nose and covered his own mouth with the collar of his coat. He leaned back into the dune, pulling his knees up to his chest. Snowy hid in the crook of Tintin's legs.

Tintin was too tired to move anymore, too tired to fight the storm.... All he could do was try to turn his back to it and hang on. It seemed to go on forever, the whistle of the wind and the stinging, scouring sand. He had sand in his eyes, in his mouth, in his ears. He felt like he was becoming a sand dune himself. Where was Snowy? He could no longer tell. "Snowy," he murmured, but his lips were chapped and his tongue was dry and the sound of Snowy's name was lost on the wind.

Sometime later, he thought he heard Snowy howling. Tintin drifted in and out of consciousness, barely aware that he was covered in sand. Was there a light? It couldn't be. They were in the middle of the desert, far from civilization. It was dark....

There *was* a light. Snowy yowled again. Tintin tried to move, but he was just...too...tired....

"Good dog!" he heard someone call out over the noise of the storm. Snowy barked.

Tintin blinked as lights swirled around him and shapes appeared in the blowing sand. "This one's alive!" he heard someone call. "Check the other!"

Someone shone a light in his face. He squinted and turned away. "Yes, sir!" another voice called through the storm. "Live one here, too!"

Snowy barked again and bounced his paws on Tintin's chest. "Good dog, Snowy," Tintin whispered.

He awoke to bright sunshine and the smell of pipe tobacco. "Ah," someone said. "You're awake. Capital."

Tintin blinked and turned over, hearing the rustle of starched sheets and realizing that he was in a bed. He was also clean, which he would not have thought possible after the past day. "I am Lieutenant Delcourt," said a uniformed chap sitting nearby. He knocked out his pipe on the heel of his boot and stood. "Welcome to the Afghar Outpost."

"Thank you, Lieutenant," Tintin said. He sat up and saw Snowy sitting near the bed, looking at him and twitching his tail.

"Fine dog you have there," Delcourt said.

"Yes, he is," Tintin said. He remembered the storm coming in, but very little after that. Afghar Outpost...where was that? How far from Bagghar? "We owe you our lives. Did you find my friend?"

146

"Yes," Delcourt said, standing. He was trim, musta-chioed...the very picture of a foreign-legion officer. "But he's not in good shape, I'm afraid. He's still suffering the effects of acute dehydration. He's quite delirious. Why don't you get dressed and we'll pay him a visit?" He went to the door and tipped his flat-topped cap. "I'll be outside."

A few minutes later, Tintin and Snowy followed Delcourt across the open ground inside the square sandstone wall surrounding the Afghar Outpost. The largest structures inside the walls were a pair of radio towers. The rest of the buildings were low and flat-roofed, mostly built right against the inside of the walls. Sentries wearing loose, flow-ing robes and head scarves patrolled the walls. Everyone except Tintin and Lieutenant Delcourt appeared to be dressed the same way. It was what people wore in this part of the world to protect themselves from the relentless sun and heat.

Near the center of the enclosure were a well and a store-house. "Before the storm hit, we saw a column of smoke on the horizon," Delcourt said. "Obviously a plane crash. It seemed the decent thing to send a search party out and look for survivors. Nightfall and the storm made it a bit more exciting."

"Thank you again, Lieutenant," Tintin said. "We crashed a seaplane."

Lieutenant Delcourt turned to him and said, "You're a lucky lad, Tintin. Very lucky. It's especially lucky that you knew how to fly a plane."

Tintin agreed that he was lucky. He didn't mention that he had only flown a plane that one time.

Lieutenant Delcourt led him and Snowy toward a non-descript building at the edge of the outpost. Delcourt opened the door and they entered, passing through a store-room piled high with everything from blankets to cannon-balls. They passed through another door into a makeshift infirmary. A couple of cots on either side of a side table lit-tered with medical equipment were the only furniture, save a battered chair in the corner that looked as if it might break when someone sat in it. Bright sunlight slanted in through two windows above the cots. The floor was bare planking, and as Tintin looked around he noticed that there was also a small table near the door. On it stood a number of small brown or clear glass bottles, similar to the medicinal spirits aboard the doomed seaplane.

Captain Haddock was there, sitting on the edge of one of the cots. He stood up as Lieutenant Delcourt entered.

Tintin thought he looked well, all things considered. The haunted look that came over him when he compared himself to previous Haddocks was gone. The desert and the storm seemed to have scoured something out of him and left him clean. *Just what he needed*, Tintin thought.

"Ah, Haddock. You're awake. Good," Delcourt said. "I have a visitor for you."

He stepped aside, revealing Tintin, as Captain Haddock turned toward the door. "Captain," Tintin said. He was happy to see Captain Haddock up and about.

But Captain Haddock's face stayed blank when he looked at Tintin, and even when he saw Snowy. "Hello!" he said, cheerfully enough. "I think you've got the wrong room."

"Captain?" Tintin repeated. Now he was starting to worry again. "It's Tintin. Our plane crashed in the desert, don't you remember?"

Haddock's brow furrowed. "Plane? No, no, I'm a naval man myself. I never fly if I can help it." To Delcourt he added, "He's got me confused with someone else."

Tintin and Delcourt exchanged glances as Captain Haddock took a sip from a glass of water on the side table by his cot. "What is this peculiar liquid?" he inquired, holding it up to the light. Snowy's ears perked up as the water cast a wavy pattern of refracted sunlight on the floor. "There's no bouquet," Captain Haddock went on. "It's completely transparent."

"Why, it's water," Lieutenant Delcourt said.

Amazed, Captain Haddock swirled it in the glass. Snowy pounced on the moving pattern of light. "What will they think of next?" Captain Haddock said.

Delcourt took Tintin's arm and turned him away from Captain Haddock so they could confer privately. "We suspect he has a concussion, heatstroke, and delirium," he said.

Tintin shook his head and walked over to Captain Haddock. He took the water glass, held it up to Delcourt, and said, "He's sober." Then, to Captain Haddock, Tintin said, "Now, Captain, out in the desert."

"The desert?" Captain Haddock repeated, as if he had never heard the word before. Tintin noticed Snowy creeping around the cot with something in his mouth, but he stayed focused on the captain.

"Yes," he said. "You were talking about Sir Francis."

Tintin sat on the cot, and Captain Haddock sat next to him. "Sir who?" he asked.

"Sir Francis," Tintin repeated patiently. "You were telling me about what happened on the *Unicorn*."

"The *Unicorn*?"

"Yes."

"The stuff that dreams are made of," Captain Haddock said. "Wee children's dreams."

"No, the ship!" Tintin said. "Please, try to remember, Captain. Lives are at stake."

Captain Haddock reached for his water glass. As he raised it to his mouth, Tintin realized that Snowy had taken matters into his own hands! Somehow Snowy had found a bottle of medicinal spirits on the table and nudged it into Captain Haddock's hand in place of the water glass, and now Captain Haddock was drinking the alcohol in one great gulp!

"Snowy!" he said. "What have you done?"

Captain Haddock's eyes bulged, then closed, and he let out a huge and satisfied sigh. "Aahhhhhhhhh."

Tintin looked back to Lieutenant Delcourt and said, "I'd stand back if I were you."

Then Captain Haddock's sigh turned into a low growl, slowly getting louder.

Uh-oh, Tintin thought.

"Out! Everybody out of the room!" he cried, jumping over the cot and scooping up Snowy on his way out the door after Lieutenant Delcourt and a group of curious soldiers who had gathered in the storeroom to peek in on the

151

strangers. He slammed the door behind him, dropping Snowy, who sprawled on the storeroom floor. A moment later, a great battle cry sounded from inside the infirmary and Captain Haddock charged through the door, breaking it into a thousand splinters.

"Show yourself, Red Rackham!" he roared, lunging as if he held a sword.

"Who is Red Rackham?" Tintin shouted. He and Delcourt rushed to get between Captain Haddock and the rest of the soldiers, who were tumbling over themselves in an effort to stay out of his way. One of them didn't move fast enough, and Captain Haddock swiftly disarmed him, jerking his sword away and shoving the soldier into his fellows. He was immersed once again in his historical vision.

He waved the sword at Tintin and the lieutenant, then craned his neck to look past them at his equally imaginary adversary. "If it's a fight you want, you've met your match!" he called out. He leaped up onto a table and assumed a fighting posture.

Tintin backed away. "A fight with who?"

"To the death, Red Rackham!" Haddock charged right off the table, and his collar caught on the wooden blade of a ceiling fan. His momentum spun the fan around before it broke. He tumbled to the floor, crashing into a barrel, and the fan landed on his head, knocking him senseless.

Tintin sprang to his aid as Lieutenant Delcourt and the other soldiers crowded around them. "Captain?" Tintin said, kneeling next to Haddock, who was slowly sitting up. Tintin relieved him of the sword and passed it to Lieutenant Delcourt, who passed it back to the soldier it belonged to.

Captain Haddock's face was ashen. "The *Unicorn* was taken," he said, quiet and sad. "Pirates were now the masters of the ship."

"The crew surrendered?" Tintin said, hoping to keep the story going.

"Granddaddy said that Red Rackham called Sir Francis the king's dog—a pirate hunter sent to reclaim their hard-won plunder." A distant light shone in Captain Haddock's eyes as he spoke, and Tintin again felt that he could almost see and hear the story that Captain Haddock told....

Lashed to the *Unicorn*'s mast by Red Rackham's men, Sir Francis glared at the masked pirate, who paraded across the deck in front of him, gloating over his triumph. His pirate crew was busy cutting loose the *Unicorn*'s tangled rigging and refitting it for their captain. Red Rackham's ship had sunk, but he would have the *Unicorn* as his prize. Sir Francis's blood boiled at the thought of his ship under the control of this villain.

Red Rackham cut a mighty figure in his scarlet cape, boots, and tall red plume, which accented the black and red of his hat. He was the best-dressed pirate on the world's oceans, and he knew it. He smirked at Sir Francis, thoughtfully stroking the points of his beard and mustache. "Now, Haddock," he said.

"Captain Sir Francis Haddock," Haddock corrected him.

"Oh, let us not insist on titles. You may call me simply Red Rackham, for that is my name," Red Rackham said. "And I care not a farthing for the cargo listed on your manifest." He held up the ship's manifest, which listed everything the *Unicorn* had taken on in Barbados before sailing. Then he tore it up and let the pieces flutter away on the breeze over the railing.

"Why would I waste my time on rum, molasses, and dates when you have a more valuable cargo on board?" He came close to Sir Francis and leaned in, face-to-face. "Where is it?"

"You'll have to kill me first," Sir Francis retorted.

An evil grin split Red Rackham's angular face, and behind his mask an evil gleam was visible in his black eyes. "Not first, no," he said. "I will start with your men...."

"No," Tintin said, back in the storeroom. "He didn't!"

Captain Haddock got up and walked around the room as if in a dream. "To save his men, Sir Francis would give up the secret cargo," he said.

"Where was it?" Tintin asked.

Reaching a bookshelf, Captain Haddock slowly pulled out a book with two fingers, as if he were pulling a secret lever. "Four hundred weight of gold, jewels, and treasure," he said. "Red Rackham got it all ... and then he killed every man aboard the *Unicorn*. He made them walk the plank, one and all. The sharks had a feast that night."

Haddock backed away from the bookshelf, still seeing something no one else in the room could see. He bumped into a table and turned, fixing his attention on an inkwell.

"Sir Francis knew he was doomed. He'd be hung from the highest yardarm at dawn, but they didn't reckon on one thing." Captain Haddock plucked a quill from the inkwell and pricked his finger with the point. "Sir Francis was a Haddock, and a Haddock always has a trick up his sleeve. The feather in Sir Francis's hat wasn't just a feather. It had a blade on the end, and he kept it always in case he would need to cut himself free from pirate ropes."

Suddenly, Haddock sprang away from the table as if he had just loosened the bonds holding his ancestor to the *Unicorn*'s mast. "He hurls himself forward!" he cried.

With a lightning motion he swept the sword from another surprised soldier's scabbard. "And seizes a cutlass!"

Then, just as quickly, he stooped and caught Snowy up in one arm, upending him and shaking him. "He makes his way to the ship's magazine, where they keep the gunpowder and the shot." He mimicked shaking a trail of gunpowder all the way from the magazine back up the stairs to the deck, using Snowy as his imaginary barrel as he backed up the stairs from the storeroom into an office on the second floor.

Tintin, Lieutenant Delcourt, and the soldiers followed, captivated by the story. Snowy looked to Tintin for help, but Tintin was too caught up to notice him.

"On the deck, Red Rackham finds him. They fight!"
Captain Haddock said. Tintin could almost see the events
unfold himself....

Swords clashed on the deck as Red Rackham and Sir Francis Haddock fought back and forth. Sir Francis defended the
trail of gunpowder, Red Rackham tried to stamp it out...
but how was Sir Francis to light it and still keep Red Rackham's cutlass out of his chest?

"Ha!" he cried, seeing a chance and taking it. Red Rackham was off balance for a moment and Sir Francis hit a
lantern with the flat of his blade. The blow shattered it, and
the burning oil fell onto the gunpowder trail. It sparked
and hissed to life, adding its smoke to the confusion on the
deck. They danced their way toward the stairs that led
down to the gun deck, Red Rackham sweeping and stamping at the gunpowder as Sir Francis knocked down lantern
after lantern, lighting the trail in a dozen different places.

Red Rackham grew more and more desperate—and in
his desperation he grew careless! Sir Francis saw an opportunity, feinting at Red Rackham's face and then plunging

his cutlass under the pirate's guard to wound him in the side. "Aargh!" Red Rackham cried. He fell back against a mast for support.

Sir Francis slashed at him again, nearly taking his head off, but at the last moment, Red Rackham dodged, and the blade slit the ribbon holding the pirate's mask over his face.

The mask fell away as the gunpowder trail burned down the stairs toward the magazine. . . .

Captain Haddock stopped. "What?" Tintin said. "What happened next?"

Around them, the soldiers leaned close, filling the office from wall to wall. Some of the soldiers had climbed onto Lieutenant Delcourt's desk to get a better view. They had been stuck out at the Afghar Outpost for a long time, and any show was a good show. Also, this one had pirates, which made it better. Tintin knew that stories were always better if they included pirates.

He also knew that Captain Haddock had been silently staring off into space for too long now for it to be just a dramatic pause. "Captain?" he said. The soldiers crowded closer, hanging on to Captain Haddock's every word.

"How could I be so blind?" Captain Haddock said.

"What are you talking about?" Tintin asked.

"This isn't just about the scrolls or the treasure," Captain Haddock said. "It's me he's after!"

"Who?" Tintin asked. "Who's after you?"

But Captain Haddock wasn't done with his story yet. The soldiers leaned in closer still; even Lieutenant Delcourt was captivated. His pipe had gone out. The last of its smoke hung over Captain Haddock, who looked as if he were back on the deck of the *Unicorn* himself, facing down his deadly enemy with fire and steel. . . .

"You'll suffer a curse on you and your name, Haddock!" shrieked the unmasked Red Rackham. Fires from the broken lanterns illuminated his scarred face, with its heavy eyebrows and nose like the blade of a knife. He charged, and the two of them tumbled down to the gun deck, separating to resume their sword fight as the gunpowder burned closer and closer to the magazine.

Sir Francis had a plan, and he executed it perfectly. Angling around between two of the *Unicorn*'s guns, he waited until the gunpowder trail had burned the length of the gun deck and disappeared into the short hall leading down to the magazine.

"A curse on your name, Haddock!" Red Rackham screamed. His wound was weakening him, and Sir Francis tipped him a wink as he got closer to one of the gun portholes. "Come back and face me!"

Smoke started to cloud the gun deck. Sir Francis knew he was out of time. . . .

"We're out of time, Tintin!" Captain Haddock screamed. He rushed to Tintin, hoisting him up and carrying him at a run to the second-story window. They crashed through it in a shower of glass, Snowy barking after them. For a moment Tintin felt weightless. Captain Haddock was shouting something in his ear.

They landed with a *whump* in a hay pile between the outbuilding and the nearby stable. Snowy scrambled up next to Tintin as he swiped hay out of his eyes and hair. For a moment Tintin thought Snowy would bite Captain Haddock, but the little dog sat at attention. His ears perked up as Captain Haddock mimed swimming, kicking up a great storm of hay. Tintin almost laughed. Snowy couldn't wait to hear how the story came out, either....

Sir Francis dove through the porthole and swam underwater as far as he could, coming up with a gasp and turning just at the moment when the *Unicorn*'s powder magazine exploded. The entire ship seemed to jump out of the water, then settle back in lower than before. Its stern was engulfed in flames, and it was sinking fast.

My ship, thought Sir Francis sadly. He climbed onto a drifting mast as a single wave lifted him and let him down again. Sir Francis realized it was the giant ripple kicked up by the explosion that had sunk the *Unicorn*. Wreckage from the explosion was falling from the night sky into the water around him. He held up his hat to protect himself from the rain of debris. And as he floated there, one arm over the mast and the other sheltering his head, he started to hear clinking from the upturned hat.

Sir Francis looked inside his hat when the debris had stopped falling. In the last light of the burning wreckage of the *Unicorn*, he saw the gleam of gold and the glint of gems....

"It's not over," Captain Haddock said softly. "It was never over." He cradled his hat in his hands. Tintin could almost imagine it as a great felt tricorne Sir Francis would have worn.

"I don't understand," Tintin said. He picked more hay out of his hair and shook his shirt. "Who's after your blood?"

"Sakharine!" Captain Haddock said.

"Sakharine!" Tintin repeated. He was shocked! But now Captain Haddock's delirious description of Red Rackham's face made sense. Nose like the blade of a knife, indeed. Angular face, yes.

"He's Red Rackham's descendant," Captain Haddock said. "He means to finish it."

"That's why he did it," Tintin said after a while. Lieutenant Delcourt and the soldiers came running around the side of the storeroom in a group; the soldiers began to disperse when they saw that the story was over. Delcourt waited politely for Tintin and Captain Haddock to finish their conversation.

Haddock looked confused. Again. "Did what?"

"Sank his own ship! Sir Francis sent that treasure to the bottom of the sea. He'd be damned before he let Red Rackham have it."

"And he was," Captain Haddock said.

"But he couldn't let it lie," Tintin went on.

"No!"

"He left a clue! Three clues wrapped in a riddle, concealing a secret. But only a true Haddock will be able to solve it. That's why they need you."

Still confused, Captain Haddock said, "What secret?"

"The location of one of the greatest sunken treasures in all of history," Tintin said. Despite himself, he was getting more and more excited. What a story this would be! The secret of the *Unicorn* was proving to be an even better mystery than he could have imagined. Tintin thought this might turn out to be his best adventure yet...if they could manage to intercept Sakharine before he got the third model ship. They had to get to Bagghar as quickly as possible. It was even more urgent now.

Finally Captain Haddock caught on to Tintin's train of thought. "The wreck of the *Unicorn*," he said. "He means to steal it. The third scroll. Billions of blue blistering barnacles, I swear as the last of the Haddocks that I'll find that treasure before he does!"

Together they leaped out of the hay pile, nearly stepping on Snowy, who barked in protest. "To Bagghar," Tintin said.

"To Bagghar!" Captain Haddock spat in his palm, and they shook hands.

It was time to see if Lieutenant Delcourt could find them a couple of fast camels.

CHAPTER 15

Three days later, they crested a sand dune just past the fabled wells of Kefheir, where they had watered their camels—and themselves. Below them spread the ancient city of Bagghar. Its white towers and minarets gleamed in the sun. From their perspective, Tintin and Captain Haddock could see the port...and in the harbor, close to the piers, they could see the *Karaboudjan* docked.

"He's here," Tintin said. "I knew it." Snowy barked in agreement from his perch on Tintin's camel.

"But we've outsmarted you, *bashi-bazouk*," Captain

Haddock growled down at the ship. "You just wait." Then he turned to Tintin. "So, what do we do?"

The city of Bagghar was laid out between the harbor and the hills, crowded in the shadow of Sheik Omar Ben Salaad's grand palace and the enormous dam above it. "The sheik cut off the water supply to the town when he built the dam," Captain Haddock explained to Tintin. "Now he sells his people the water, but says he keeps taxes low."

"That sneak," Tintin said. He studied the layout of Bagghar, seeing the single winding road that led from the palace down into what must have once been a riverbed. But since Ben Salaad had taken the river away, it was a dry canyon between the base of the dam and the inland edge of Bagghar proper. From there to the ocean, a canal ran away from the winding riverbed straight through the middle of town.

The palace itself was an extraordinary piece of architecture. It was terraced right into the steep bluffs at the base of the dam and surrounded by lush gardens, in contrast to the parched redness of the hills around it. Its white stone walls gleamed fiercely in the Moroccan sun, and from the tops of its many towers flew Ben Salaad's personal flag. A thousand people could have slept on its grounds, thought

Tintin, and had room to stretch out and roll over. In contrast, the main part of Bagghar was a jumble and tangle of low buildings, jostling for space in the lowlands between the palace and the brilliant blue-green water of Bagghar's excellent harbor.

He couldn't believe that Ben Salaad would steal water from his own people and sell it back to them. If there was any justice in the world, they would be able to do something about it—but that was another story, for another time. Tintin had to focus on the story at hand, and that was the secret of the *Unicorn*.

"What's the plan, Tintin?" Captain Haddock asked.

Tintin shook his head. "We don't have enough information to make a good plan yet," he said. "We need to look around first."

"Then let's get looking!"

Tintin and Captain Haddock rode down into town quickly. They needed to get there before Sakharine could establish spies in the town to keep watch for them. As they rode through the outskirts of Bagghar, people called to them, thinking that because they had come through the desert they must be traders. Also, everyone seemed to be looking for water. Signs all over town proclaimed CONSERVE

WATER in all the languages Tintin and Captain Haddock could read and in some they couldn't. As they took in the parched surroundings, a sharp-looking man with a pointy mustache and a wad of bills in his hand stepped out from an enclosure full of camels. Over the fence was a sign printed in several languages: USED CAMELS CHEAP AND RELIABLE!

"You sell your camel, *effendi*?" the camel dealer asked. He riffled the bills in his hand.

"Make me an offer," Captain Haddock replied. They quickly sold the tired camels in exchange for some cash.

From there, walking through the streets, they cut toward the port looking for Sakharine or his men. Snowy sniffed for familiar scents, but everything was foreign to him. He sneezed at the dust. Many of the people in Bagghar wore scarves over their faces, which made them difficult to identify or recognize, but Tintin had lots of experience identifying people. He quickly suspected that he had seen some of the same people more than once.

Everywhere, there were long lines of townsfolk waiting to get water from pumps, standing in line for hours just for a splash of the precious liquid. Every square in the town had a pump, but not much water came out of them. Tintin couldn't believe such hardship existed when there was a large reservoir not five miles away. Looking at the towns-people of Bagghar, anyone would have thought that the nearest river was a hundred miles away.

"Captain, we must do something about this," he said.

"Aye, lad," Captain Haddock said agreeably as they walked through a plaza. At its center stood a dry fountain. Children played in it, but it had been a long time since any of them had splashed around. Tintin's mind spun as he thought up plan after plan and then discarded each one. How could they get into the palace and escape with the third *Unicorn*?

And even if they did, how was he going to reclaim his wallet, which held the first scroll?

They walked close to a long breakwater that jutted out from the waterfront. At the end of it, the *Karaboudjan* lay at anchor, but there was no sign of Sakharine, Allan, Tom, or anyone else from the ship. "Captain," Tintin said. "We know they're going to see the Milanese Nightingale, or else why would they have had the brochure in the radio room? Maybe we should head toward the palace."

Turning away from the harbor, they plunged back into the town of Bagghar. They saw thirsty people everywhere... but they did not see any of the people they were looking for.

Captain Haddock was complaining as they reached a main square again. The dry fountain was ahead of them, and beyond it the main bazaar of Bagghar. The palace loomed to their left, in the shadow of the immense dam. "They could be anywhere!" Captain Haddock said.

Tintin leaned close to him and said, "Don't look now, but we're being followed."

A conspiratorial expression came over Captain Haddock's face. They kept walking, and he slowly glanced behind him. "Ah," he said, facing forward again. "So we are."

They cut through the marketplace toward the palace of Ben Salaad. "Action?" Tintin suggested.

"Why, yes," Captain Haddock agreed. "Action is most definitely called for."

They ducked into an alley leading away from the main open bazaar and quickly stepped inside an open doorway. Snowy peered around the door and then backed up between them, thumping his tail. "That means they're coming," Tintin explained to Captain Haddock.

"Good dog," Captain Haddock said.

A moment later the first of the two hooded figures whom Tintin had spotted came strolling past the doorway. Tintin stuck out a foot and tripped him. The man sprawled onto the dusty ground, and the second man fell, too!

Tintin jumped out, clenching his fists. "Why are you following us?" he demanded.

Captain Haddock took things a step further, leaping on both of them and pounding them into the ground quite ferociously. "Who are you working for?" he yelled, as if either of them could have answered while he flailed away with his fists.

Their hoods slipped back at the same time, and Tintin could have fallen over from surprise when he saw two identical bowler hats!

"Captain, stop!" he cried, wading into the struggle to pull Haddock back. "It's Thompson and Thomson!" The hats fell away in the rumpus, and Captain Haddock managed to step on both of them.

He helped the battered detectives to their feet. "Not so loud," Thomson said. He punched his hat back into shape and resettled it on his head.

Thompson's hat was also a bit crumpled. He popped the worst of the dimples out and added, "We're in disguise."

Tintin nodded. "So I see. You got the message I sent from the ship?"

Counting on them had been part of his plan from the moment he saw the wireless transmitter on board the *Karaboudjan*. He was glad to see the two Interpol detectives here in

171

Bagghar—now they could even the odds a little bit. Thompson and Thomson were bumblers sometimes, but when the chips were down, Tintin knew he could count on them.

"Yes, well, bit of a long story there," Thompson said.

"The upshot is we caught the pickpocket, retrieved your wallet, and hopped on the next plane to Bagghar," Thomson said.

The detectives exchanged glances then, and Tintin had a feeling there was more to the story than they were letting on.

"Yes," Thompson said. "That pocket picker has picked his last pocket." With a flourish, he produced Tintin's wallet. "Don't worry. He didn't take any money."

"It's not the money I'm worried about," Tintin said as he opened the wallet, turning away from everyone to see for himself whether the parchment was safe. His fingers dipped into the interior flap where he had hidden it...and there it was!

Turning back to Captain Haddock and the detectives, he said, "The odds are even!"

As they walked back toward the marketplace, Tintin saw a large banner hanging above the square. All of a sudden he had a plan. "The Milanese Nightingale," he said.

The others looked up and read the banner, which was mostly occupied by a dramatic portrait of the Milanese Nightingale herself. Apparently, she was an opera singer; her actual name was Bianca Castafiore. Tintin thought it was a very dramatic portrait. Below it, the banner announced her appearance at the great hall of Ben Salaad's palace. She was to sing that very evening!

"Ahh, what a dish," Captain Haddock said.

"Quite," Thompson and Thomson agreed.

Tintin had other things on his mind. The thirsty townspeople of Bagghar stood in line for water from a pump near the empty fountain, talking about the concert. It sounded as if every one of them was planning to go. The scene at Ben Salaad's palace would be chaotic—the perfect time to pull off a heist of a valuable antique like the third model *Unicorn*. *But what about the display case?* Tintin wondered. How did Sakharine propose to get through the bulletproof glass?

Again, he looked up at the banner and its portrait of the Milanese Nightingale. "That's his secret weapon?" he asked incredulously. But the more he thought about it, the more sense it made. He was beginning to believe he knew how Sakharine planned to capture the third model *Unicorn*. Tintin had to get there first.

Sakharine probably had friends in the palace and a posse of armed thugs who would do anything he wanted. Tintin had the two detectives, Captain Haddock, and Snowy.

The difference, however, was that Tintin was chasing the mystery. He knew there was treasure to be found, but he didn't care too much about it. It was the mystery that drew him onward. Where was this treasure? What was the secret of the *Unicorn*?

The only way he was ever going to find out was if he stopped Sakharine and captured all three scrolls.

"The concert is happening tonight," Tintin said. "We must get to the palace immediately."

Outside Ben Salaad's grand palace, Tintin found a manic scene. Reporters were shouting over one another, paparazzi were shooting a million pictures, and fans of the Milanese Nightingale were crowding against the velvet ropes clamoring for autographs. The entire city seemed to have traveled to the palace courtyard to get in on the show. Bianca Castafiore, the Nightingale herself, was a large and imposing figure in an emerald silk gown covered in sparkling gold brocade. Her blond hair was swept into a complicated knot. Diamonds sparkled in her ears and at her throat.

"She would have been a fine figurehead on the *Unicorn* herself," Captain Haddock said, marveling at her. It was the greatest compliment a Haddock could give.

From the back of the crowd, in the shadow of the looming grand hall, Tintin took note of the garage and driveway at one side of the palace, and identified all the outside doors. At some point, he was going to have to make a quick getaway, and he wanted options. Surveying the grounds, Tintin was again struck by the difference between the palace grounds and the rest of the town. Inside Ben Salaad's walls, everything was lush and green, perfectly groomed and flowering. Fountains and decorative canals cut here and there alongside stone sidewalks. The air was fragrant with flowers and freshly mowed grass.

Outside the walls, dead grass and brown struggling shrubs stuck up out of parched earth. The entire town looked as if the water had been squeezed out of it long ago. Tintin felt sorry for the people of Bagghar. He vowed to do what he could to bring justice to them. Sheik Ben Salaad had to be forced to acknowledge that what he was doing was wrong.

But their first objective was to capture the third scroll.

The Nightingale smiled and smiled at everyone, posing for photograph after photograph. Handing back an autographed program, she laughed at something someone said, and the laugh rose to a trill that would have hurt Tintin's ears if there hadn't been so much other noise already.

At her side stood Ben Salaad himself, bespectacled and a little mousy-looking, sporting a wispy mustache on a round, soft face. One would not have taken him for the rich and powerful man he was. He made a great show of bowing and kissing her hand. The photographers clicked away. "Enchanted, *signora*," Ben Salaad said. "*Bienvenuto!* Welcome! We are blessed with your presence."

"Yes, indeed, *Signore* Salad," the Nightingale said, mispronouncing her host's name. He did not appear to notice, and she kept waving to the crowd. "What charming peasants!" she said, more quietly. Tintin read her lips as she leaned in close to Ben Salaad and said, "May I introduce my escort, Monsieur Shuggair Addeitiff...?"

And from behind her stepped Sakharine, dressed in a tailored tuxedo!

176

The photographers kept snapping pics. Between Tintin's feet, Snowy growled. Captain Haddock growled, too.

"He has been very passionate in his support of this concert," the Nightingale said, raising her voice again so the whole crowd could hear. "It's my first visit to this part of the world."

"Please forgive me," Sakharine said, bowing to Ben Salaad. "I must escort Madame to her dressing room. Excuse us!"

He and the Nightingale entered the palace to a final chorus of questions from the assembled reporters. Tintin had a few questions of his own.

But they would have to wait. For now, he and Captain Haddock applauded along with the rest of the crowd as Ben Salaad and his secretary shouted, "Bravo!" over and over again to the retreating Nightingale and her sinister escort.

The money in Tintin's wallet, plus what they had received from the sale of the camels, was enough for two tickets to the opera. Tintin and Captain Haddock got themselves cleaned up as best they could and a little while later were waiting in line to enter for the performance. Tintin watched the palace guards keeping an eye on everyone who went inside. He got worried that maybe Sakharine might have told the guards to look out for him, and on the spur of the moment he made a decision.

He took the scroll from his wallet and handed it to Captain Haddock. "Here," he said. "I want you to look after this."

"Me? Are you sure?" Captain Haddock looked uncomfortable.

"I think they're watching me," Tintin said. "If I'm caught, I don't want them to find this on me. Just keep it hidden."

Captain Haddock dramatically dropped to one knee, clasping the folded parchment to his heart. "I will guard this with my life!"

"No, no," Tintin said, pulling him back up. The last thing he wanted was Captain Haddock making a scene and drawing attention to himself. "Shh. Just keep it safe."

Then they were passing close to the guards. Tintin tried not to look at them, and also tried not to look nervous. Captain Haddock stood stiffly, looking like he had just swallowed a sea urchin. But the guards took no notice of them, and an usher escorted them to their seats. Snowy stealthily padded in under the cover of a lady's skirt. He didn't need a ticket!

They were far from the stage, toward the back of the main floor of the hall. On either side of the floor rose decks of special boxes, and two balconies jutted out over the display area at the back of the hall. Tintin needed opera glasses to see anything, and luckily they were being handed out for free to all of the distinguished guests. Ben Salaad was in the first row, dead center. The great hall of his palace was alive with excitement. Every dignitary in Bagghar, and quite a few of the Nightingale's traveling fans, had packed into the hall for this unprecedented show. The orchestra struck up the overture to a famous opera, and a hush came over the hall as the lights dimmed save for a single spotlight shining on Bianca Castafiore at center stage.

"It's her!" Captain Haddock said, poking Tintin with his elbow. It seemed the captain was already quite a fan.

Tintin had his opera glasses out and was panning through the crowd. He stopped when he had the display case containing the third model *Unicorn* in view. It was near the doors at the rear of the hall, below the overhang of the first balcony. Where was Sakharine? How was he planning to get it?

Tintin wished he could have gotten Thompson and Thomson into the concert, but both of them had felt that they would be of more use out in the town. They had pledged to make sure that Tintin got back to Europe once he had achieved his objective, but neither of them wanted to attend the performance. Tintin had a feeling that they were not opera fans.

The overture came to a climax and died away, and the Milanese Nightingale began to sing. She had a huge voice, that much could not be denied — but Captain Haddock was clearly not prepared for what he heard. He looked horrified as the first notes of the Nightingale's high-pitched aria drilled into his ears.

"Blistering barnacles, what's that noise?" He clapped his hands to the sides of his head. "My ears! They're bleeding!"

"No, they're not," Tintin scoffed. Haddock didn't seem to hear. He bent forward and banged his head against the chair in front of him. On the floor at Tintin's feet, Snowy began to whine. Nobody other than Tintin could have heard him, so loud was the Nightingale's voice.

She began to climb to the higher notes in the middle of the aria, and Tintin's ears started to ring. "Oh, Columbus!" Captain Haddock cried. "It's every man for himself!"

He stood and pushed his way up the aisle past annoyed patrons, crying out, "Make way, make way! Medical emergency!"

When he was out in the lobby, Captain Haddock breathed a sigh of relief. He could still hear the accursed noise from inside the hall, but at least it was muffled by the doors. *Time for a little relief*, he thought, removing a medicinal spirit bottle from his jacket pocket.

As it came out, so did the scroll Tintin had given him. "Whoops," said Captain Haddock. He snatched it out of the air and folded it up again, holding it tight in his fist.

"Whew," he said. He started to open the bottle. . . .

Then he paused. Tintin had trusted him with this scroll. He had to live up to that trust. And he was a Haddock! He came from a long line of sea captains and mighty adventurers!

He didn't need the bottle.

A great sense of peace came over Captain Haddock, and he put the bottle down on a marble-topped table at the edge of the lobby. As he took a step away from it, someone stepped in front of him. Haddock looked up and gasped.

"Hello, Captain," Tom said.

"You!" Captain Haddock said. He spun around, and there was Sakharine's other goon, Allan. Before Captain Haddock could move, Allan snatched up the bottle and brought it crashing down on Captain Haddock's head.

CHAPTER 16

Tintin leaned forward, his anticipation growing as the Milanese Nightingale approached the climax of her song. From the corner of his eye, Tintin saw something move that distracted him. He glanced up at the upper balcony, feeling uneasy, just as a figure disappeared from view. And there had been another motion...what was it?

He picked up the opera glasses and scanned the balcony. Suddenly, he saw him! Sakharine!

The notes of the Nightingale's aria went higher still. "Oh, no," Tintin said. His musings had been right. From around him came the sharp tinkle of breaking glass as the power of the Nightingale's voice began to shatter the guests' champagne glasses—and even the lenses of their spectacles.

That was Sakharine's plan, thought Tintin. The woman onstage could sing notes so high that they shattered glass!

From the balcony, he saw a flutter. A flutter? Yes. Sakharine's falcon! It was a great majestic bird. It tensed its wings, as if prepared to take flight at any moment.

A glass chandelier shattered into fragments that rained down into the waiting area behind the seats. Along the wall of that waiting area stood the display case holding the model ship. Cracks were spreading across the bulletproof glass as the Nightingale's voice soared higher and higher. The lenses of Tintin's opera glasses cracked and fell out of the casing.

Tintin stood. It was time to act!

The Nightingale raised her arms, summoning all her strength to hit the final notes...

...and the display case shattered, shards of glass spilling across the expensive plush carpeting of the waiting area. Urgently, Tintin started pushing through the crowd toward the aisle. Down in the front row, Ben Salaad heard the crash even over the onslaught of the Nightingale's voice. He looked over his shoulder and saw Sakharine lean forward with a smile as he launched the falcon from the balcony.

"The falcon!" Tintin cried. "Snowy, after it!"

Snowy slipped under the seats and took off. At the same moment, Captain Haddock burst in from the lobby, shouting, "Tintin!"

Mad applause was breaking out for the Nightingale even as Sakharine leaned out over the balcony and pointed at Captain Haddock and Tintin, using both hands. "Those two!" he yelled over the din to Ben Salaad. "They're here to steal your ship!"

Ben Salaad leaped up and fought his way up the aisle from the front row, waving his arms and shouting orders that Tintin couldn't hear. "No, no, no, we're not!" Tintin protested.

"Arrest him!" Ben Salaad shouted, pointing at Captain Haddock. "The ugly one!"

The audience was confused. Some of them still applauded while others were following this new drama. At Tintin's side, an old man in military dress, his chest spangled with medals, put a hand on Tintin's arm.

Tintin shook him off and started pushing toward the aisle. "No, wait!" he cried.

In the back of the hall, Captain Haddock saw Ben Salaad pointing. The captain pointed at himself and asked, "Me?"

"Yes!" Ben Salaad raged. "Thief! Arrest him!"

Soldiers rushed toward the puzzled Captain Haddock. On the stage, the Milanese Nightingale looked confused by the chaos. She was not accustomed to people paying attention to other things during her standing ovations. But out in the great hall of Ben Salaad's palace there was a falcon swooping, a little white dog swerving through the legs of startled patrons, Ben Salaad himself shouting and waving his arms, and a group of soldiers converging on an unkempt man in the back of the hall.

"*C'est un voleur!*" the sheik shouted as his soldiers tackled Captain Haddock en masse. Captain Haddock roared and fought back, fists flying. Soldiers went down in every direction. Through it all, the Milanese Nightingale continued to take her bows.

Tintin had reached the aisle and was elbowing his way through the crowd in the direction of Captain Haddock, but he was also trying to keep an eye on Sakharine and the falcon, which even then was diving down toward the shattered case. "Snowy!" Tintin called, and Snowy burst out of the crowd in a white blur.

The falcon picked up the *Unicorn* model and quickly dropped it. With a crash it hit the floor and the tiny mast broke. The falcon swooped back around, with Snowy bearing down on the model. A tiny metal cylinder fell out of the broken mast and rolled across the floor.

The falcon reached down with its talons.

Snowy reached up with his jaws.

The falcon snatched up the cylinder and beat its wings, rising back into the air just ahead of Snowy's leap. Snowy snapped at its tail feathers before falling back to the floor and barking furiously. All Tintin could do was watch as the falcon soared back up to Sakharine, who reached out to take the cylinder. He caught Tintin's eye and shot him a mocking wink. Then he disappeared into the back of the balcony. Over the whole scene, Ben Salaad shouted orders in French.

Tintin got to Captain Haddock, and together the two of them cleared a path through Ben Salaad's guards to the door. They escaped into the halls of the palace. "Sakharine's got the scroll!" Tintin said breathlessly.

"It's worse than that!" Haddock said. "They took your scroll, too, Tintin! It's gone!"

Tintin came to a skidding halt. Back down the corridor,

he could hear the shouts of pursuit, but they were not yet too close. He got his bearings and realized that he was close to the garage. From there he could get a car or something. He would catch Sakharine yet!

And now that Captain Haddock had lost the scroll, catching Sakharine was more urgent than ever. "How?" he asked. "What happened?"

"It was Allan," Captain Haddock said. "He—he knobbled me in the—in the... garden?"

Tintin ran down the corridor toward the outside door, disappointed in the captain. Luckily, he had a chance to take out his disappointment on one of Ben Salaad's guards, who stood between him and one of the palace's many courtyards. He knocked out the guard and then looked around to see if he could get a sense of which way Sakharine might have gone.

Then he saw a motorcycle. *Aha!* Tintin thought. At the same time he remembered that from the palace, only one road led back down to Bagghar, past the spillway gate at the base of the dam. So there was only one way Sakharine could have gone.

"Tintin!" Captain Haddock burst out of the palace and ran across the courtyard toward him. "Where are you going?"

188

"I'm going after Sakharine," Tintin said.

Haddock frowned in confusion. "By yourself?"

"Yes," Tintin said. "Come on, Snowy." Tintin hopped onto the motorcycle and fired it up. He glanced over to see if Snowy was in the sidecar, and to his surprise he saw Captain Haddock knocking out the guard (who was just getting up again) with the guard's own weapon (a bazooka!).

The motorcycle rocked as Captain Haddock leaped into the sidecar with the rocket launcher. "What are you bringing that thing for?" Tintin asked.

"You never know!" cried Captain Haddock as they roared out of the courtyard toward the main driveway that Sakharine must have taken on his way through town to the *Karaboudjan*. Snowy ran after them, barking, and made the jump into Captain Haddock's lap as Tintin slowed to take the first sharp curve in the driveway.

They caught Sakharine much sooner than Tintin would have expected, barely halfway down the winding road from the palace to Bagghar proper. He couldn't believe his good luck. Tom was driving a jeep with Sakharine in the passenger seat and Allan in the back. Allan, unfortunately, had a machine gun. As soon as he saw Tintin,

189

Allan started filling the air around the motorcycle with bullets.

Snowy huddled in the bottom of the sidecar, and Tintin ducked lower behind the handlebars of the motorcycle, making himself a smaller target. He gunned the motorcycle and started to close the distance between them and the jeep. When someone was shooting at you and escape was impossible, the only thing to do was turn the tables and go after them!

Captain Haddock had a similar idea. He braced himself in the sidecar and swung the rocket launcher up onto his shoulder. He was hollering something, but Tintin couldn't hear over the racket of the engines and the gunfire and the wind. He thought he heard the name *Red Rackham*. He looked over at Captain Haddock, hoping the captain hadn't gotten lost in one of his hallucinations again.

With a loud whoosh, the rocket launcher fired. Tintin was looking forward again, keeping them on the road. He didn't see the rocket, or a trail of smoke...or an impact....

"Did you hit anything?" he yelled.

He glanced over again to see Captain Haddock and

Snowy both looking backward. "Oh," Captain Haddock said. "Yes."

Captain Haddock threw away the rocket launcher. Tintin looked over his shoulder and put two and two together as he saw a tiny plume of smoke at the edge of the spillway gate.

"Uh-oh," he said. Captain Haddock had shot the rocket backward, launching it toward the dam!

The dam burst with a sound like rolling thunder. A tower of water churned past the palace wall and roared into the riverbed and the head of the empty canal. Tintin gunned the motorcycle again, closing in on Sakharine's jeep and also staying just ahead of the flood.

They were in Bagghar now, zigzagging through its streets. Tintin could hear Sakharine up ahead screaming at Tom to go faster. At the side of the road, the canal was filling—too high! In places the surge of water had overspilled the banks. Water swirled in the streets around them. The jeep had to slow down to take a corner, and Tintin shot up next to it.

Snowy jumped over to the other vehicle, snapping his teeth at the scrolls, which Sakharine clutched in one bony hand. Sakharine lifted them away from Snowy—practically handing them to Tintin, who sang out, "Thank you!" and grabbed them. Tintin tried to steer with one hand, keeping pace with the water that was surging into Bagghar's canals. Snowy used the jeep's rear seat as a springboard and leaped back into the sidecar.

They reached the main square just as the fountain gushed back to life, water shooting thirty feet and higher into the air. The people of Bagghar cheered and danced in the water as Tintin shot past them, Sakharine's jeep in hot pursuit. Other villagers carrying jugs and bottles ran from every direction into the square. *Ha!* Tintin thought. *We didn't mean to, but we managed to get the people of Bagghar their water. Ben Salaad will control them no longer!*

Sakharine's falcon flew out of the jeep and swooped down toward Tintin as he veered the motorcycle away. Tom was saying all kinds of impolite things as he fought to control the jeep in the crowd and the water that was starting to pour into the street. Tintin thought they were going to get away free and clear, but at that moment a wall next to the road collapsed and a tank slid through, its treads grinding the wall to dust and pebbles, which were then swept away in the flood.

A tank?! Ben Salaad means business, Tintin thought.

The tank's long gun barrel clonked Captain Haddock on the head. Tintin swerved to avoid hitting the tank, but he was shocked when Captain Haddock was jerked up and out of the sidecar! The sea captain's wool coat had been snagged by the tank's gun barrel. The sudden motion also made the three scrolls slip from Tintin's hand!

Captain Haddock grabbed two of them as they fluttered past him. "Tintin, I've lost one!" he cried out.

Snowy came to the rescue, twisting in the air to snap up the third scroll before it could be lost to the wind and chaos. "Nice work, Snowy," Tintin said.

The tank careened down the narrow streets with Captain Haddock still dangling from its turret gun. Incredibly, that tank also seemed to be dragging an entire building behind it. It was a hotel! People trapped inside leaned out their windows and screamed at the tank.

Captain Haddock was yelling, too. "Where'd you get your driver's license?" he raged as he banged into walls and doorways on either side of the street. Tintin tried to stay close so Captain Haddock would have a place to fall when he got himself loose, but the road narrowed and he had to gun the motorcycle ahead again.

The tank's gun suddenly fired with an ear-splitting boom. The shell blasted through the link between the motorcycle and sidecar, sending the sidecar—with Snowy still in it!—rolling off down a side street while Tintin stayed perilously close to the tank. The firing of the shot knocked Captain Haddock loose. He swung like a monkey along clotheslines strung between buildings before thumping down to the street in a storm of falling laundry.

Somehow, he came up from the pile of clothes wearing a pink dress, but this didn't stop Captain Haddock. His skirt rippling, he ran off after one of the scrolls that had gotten loose in the fall. It was fluttering and twisting through the air toward the canal!

"Tintin, there goes number two!" he cried out.

He ran along the canal wall as Tintin and the jeep played cat-and-mouse through the streets nearby. Almost there! The scroll dipped close and Captain Haddock lunged after it, but the falcon swooped in and snatched it from his fingertips. "Come back, you pilfering parakeet!" Captain Haddock yelled. He chased the bird along the wall and suddenly noticed Snowy, still in the sidecar, riding the surge of water in the canal itself. "Snowy!" Captain Haddock called out. "Get the scroll!"

At that moment, Tintin got close enough to swerve right next to the wall. "Captain!" he shouted. Captain Haddock, still at a dead run, jumped from the wall onto the motorcycle's handlebars.

"The bird, Captain!" he yelled in Haddock's ear. They were closing in, with water rushing all around them. The falcon was struggling against crazy winds whipped up by the flood, and Tintin thought they just might be able to catch it before it got too much altitude. He looked around. Where was Sakharine?

Just ahead of them, Snowy surfed the rushing water right to the falcon. It was starting to gain altitude, but Snowy pounced before it could get away! He pinned the falcon between his paws on the edge of the sidecar and seized the scroll in his teeth without dropping the one he already had in his mouth. The dog and bird began to fight a violent tug-of-war. "Nice work, Snowy!" Tintin said. "Don't let him go!"

Captain Haddock leaned out from the motorcycle, reaching for the falcon. It was too far. He got his balance and jumped, aiming to land in the sidecar, but he missed ever so slightly. All his weight came down on the edge of the sidecar, catapulting Snowy and the falcon straight up in the air!

The falcon flapped with all its might to get away as Snowy still held the other end of the scroll in his teeth.

"You burglarizing, budgering, jackal-eyed jackdaw!" Captain Haddock roared. "Hang on, Snowy, I'm—"

Captain Haddock's voice trailed off as the flood carried him through the open window of another building. Snowy and the falcon crashed into the wall. The water rose and the falcon kept flapping, but Snowy held on. Captain Haddock caught another dangling clothesline and swung up into a high window of a nearby tower. He caught Snowy's leg, but it startled the terrier so much that his jaws slipped and he let go of both scrolls! Now the bird had two scrolls, one in its beak and one in its talons. Captain Haddock and Snowy sprinted through the tower to the other side, just missing the bird as it swooped out another window.

Tintin on his motorcycle and Sakharine in the jeep jockeyed through the streets below. Bagghar was coming to life. Everywhere, people were running around and celebrating the return of water to the town. It was a fine sight to see, but it made for tricky driving.

Looking up, Tintin saw Captain Haddock dive partway out of one of the tower's upper windows after the falcon. Reaching, he lost the third scroll! "Noo!" Haddock shouted as the falcon banked around and calmly snatched the precious parchment out of the air.

Sakharine called to the falcon, which wheeled in his direction. He was at the edge of the bazaar near the main square. The tank rumbled somewhere nearby, still dragging the hotel through the streets and knocking pieces off other buildings.

Just as the falcon reached Sakharine, Tintin gunned the motorcycle's engine and crashed right through a spice seller's stall nearby. A cloud of spices covered them, and everyone sneezed explosively — except Tintin, who had covered his nose! Even the bird was sneezing. Tintin took advantage of the chaos to grab two of the scrolls, but as he reached for the third, the falcon got away from him and flew in the direction of the harbor. He went after it.

At that moment, Captain Haddock, who had been leaping across rooftops with Snowy right behind him, plunged down from a nearby building into the enemy's jeep. "Bashibazouks!" he roared. "Mutineers!" He laid into the sneezing Tom and Allan with his fists, pummeling them. "Ah, Mr. Allan!" he said. "You ship-stealing parasite. Allow me to return the favor!"

The vehicle jerked forward and roared off despite Captain

Haddock's best efforts. He grappled with Allan as Tom tried to keep the jeep under control while dodging stray punches from both of them. Sakharine swiveled around, looking for his falcon.

Tintin was hot on the bird's trail. The chase carried him into a house built on stilts near the harbor, and he rode the motorcycle up the front steps and through the front door. He crashed into a living room and saw the falcon get tangled up in threads trailing out from a loom in one corner. The falcon flapped and struggled free, but with stray threads clinging to its feathers, it bobbled in the air. "Excuse me! Pardon me!" Tintin called out to the surprised occupants of the apartment. He accelerated out the window on the other side of the building, hitting the back wall hard enough that the entire house fell over and split open like an egg.

The motorcycle zoomed up a flight of stairs, smashing into a stone wall. Rebounding from the impact, Tintin caught one of its handlebars as it flew off the crashed bike. He strung it on telephone wires and rode them like a zip line, following the falcon, which trailed wisps of spun cotton.

As he ran out of phone line, Tintin jumped off into the

nearest window, and found himself in an apartment. He dashed through the apartment, keeping pace with the thread-tangled falcon as he passed each window. He burst out onto a balcony and saw the falcon dropping one wing, just beginning to bank away from the building. Tintin knew he would lose the bird if he didn't act fast.

There was only one thing to do.

He leaped onto the balcony railing, sprang out into the air—and caught the falcon in the midst of its turn!

He landed with a grunt on a wooden platform. Somehow, the chase had led them to the harbor. Seawater lapped at the pilings that supported the platform. The bird fought, but Tintin held on. There wasn't a moment to waste. He had all three scrolls now, even though the falcon wouldn't let the third go. That was all right. He held the bird in one spot and put the other two scrolls next to the one it held. "Hidden numbers," he said to himself as he got the three scrolls aligned and saw...

"I wouldn't do that if I were you!" called Sakharine's voice.

Tintin looked up and saw that Tom and Allan had captured Captain Haddock. They held him out over a long drop from a nearby building. They had Snowy, too. He dangled from a rope tied to Captain Haddock's waist. Below them, the harbor churned at the mouth of the canal, clogged with wreckage and mud.

"Let the bird go," Sakharine demanded. "What do you value more, those scrolls or Haddock's life?"

"Don't listen to him!" Haddock shouted. "You'll never get away with this, you sour-faced sassinack!"

"I will kill him!" Sakharine threatened.

Tintin held on to the falcon. He had a plan, but he wasn't sure it would work. One thing he did know was that Sakharine's goons were going to drop Captain Haddock no matter what Tintin did. That was the problem with being a villain, he thought. Nobody believed you when you said you would make a fair trade.

"Let the bird go now or this man dies!" Sakharine threatened.

"No, wait!" Tintin said. He was so close. So close... the crucial clue was literally in his hands!

Dangling from the balcony, Captain Haddock raged on. "You two-timing troglodyte! You simpering son of a profiteer!"

I just need one more moment, Tintin thought... but he wasn't going to get it. "Here's mud in your eye!" Sakharine gloated. Tom and Allan let go of Captain Haddock, who plunged downward toward the muddy water.

"Fathead!" Captain Haddock roared, and disappeared into the harbor. Snowy splashed in a split second later.

With a cry of frustration, Tintin let the falcon go and dove in after them.

When the flood had calmed, the entire town of Bagghar was celebrating. Its canals were full of sparkling fresh water. The river flowed down its natural course, winding its way from the blown spillway to the sea. Sheik Ben Salaad's palace was partially in ruins, some of its walls undercut by the initial flood. The people of Bagghar were jubilant. They had water! They had fresh water for the first time since... how long had it been?

The hotel caught on the back of the tank had come to rest at the edge of the beach when the tank had run out of gas. The hotelier was painting BEACHFRONT ACCESS on the sign at that very moment as his guests took in the fine view from their windows. Among the guests were Thompson and Thomson, who were just then turning to each other and saying, "You always wanted to go to the beach."

These were the conversations going on around them as Tintin and Captain Haddock sat on the beach watching the *Karaboudjan* steam out into the bay. Captain Haddock was purple with rage. *"Nobody steals my ship!"*

"They already have," Tintin said dejectedly.

After a pause to think this over, Captain Haddock said, "Nobody takes my ship *twice*!"

The *Karboudjan*'s horn sounded, the blast rolling across the bay as the ship made the wide turn around the harbor's breakwater toward open ocean.

"We'll show them, eh, won't we, Tintin?" Captain Haddock said. He seemed manic with an optimism Tintin couldn't understand. "All right, then, what's the plan?"

"There is no plan," Tintin said.

"Of course there's a plan," Haddock said. "You've always got to have a plan."

"Not this time," Tintin said.

Haddock just looked at him, as if expecting a punch line.

"Sakharine has the scrolls," Tintin said. "They'll lead him to the treasure. It could be anywhere in the world. We'll never see him again. It's over."

"I thought you were an optimist!" Captain Haddock yelled.

"Well, you were wrong, weren't you?" Tintin said. "I'm a realist."

Captain Haddock braced his fists against his hips. "That's just another name for a quitter."

"You can call it what you like. Don't you get it? We failed." He sank his chin into his hands and looked out over the water. The *Karaboudjan* had nearly completed its maneuver around the breakwater. They had lost. Tintin was deep in self-pity. After coming all this way, he would never find the answer to the mystery. The secret of the *Unicorn* was lost to him forever.

"Failed?" Captain Haddock echoed. "There are plenty of people out there who'll call you a failure. A fool, a loser, a hopeless souse! But don't you ever say it of yourself!"

He sat next to Tintin on a chair that had washed out of one of the buildings in town. Tintin could feel Haddock looking at him.

"You send out the wrong signal, that's what people pick up, understand?" Captain Haddock went on. "You care about something, you fight for it. You hit a wall, you push through it."

He stood up again, on fire with nervous energy, and walked a short distance away. The *Karaboudjan* was farther away now, lost to them along with the secrets it carried. "There's something you need to know about failure, Tintin," Captain Haddock said. "You can never let it defeat you."

Something in that avalanche of words got through the fog of gloom surrounding Tintin. He tried to replay what Captain Haddock had said, but kept getting lost. "What did you just say?" he asked.

"You hit a wall, you push through it!" Captain Haddock answered.

"No, you said something about...sending out a signal!" Everything snapped into focus, and Tintin stood up, slapping the sand from his trousers and hands. "Of course! I sent a radio message from the *Karaboudjan*. I know what frequency they use!"

Now it was Haddock's turn to be confused. "How does that help us?"

"All we have to do is get the information to Interpol," Tintin said. "They can track the signals and work out which way the *Karaboudjan* is heading."

"Interpol," Captain Haddock said, as if the word were somehow magic.

"Interpol," Tintin said, pointing down the beach.

Captain Haddock turned to look, and both of them watched as Thompson and Thomson walked out the front door of the now-beachfront hotel and promptly fell next to each other in the sand. "Any port the ship enters, we'll know at once," Tintin said.

Haddock looked up and down the beach. He spotted a seaplane, rocking gently at its mooring in shallow water. He clapped his hands. "And we can get there first!"

CHAPTER 17

Sakharine inhaled the fishy salt air of the docks as he strode down the gangway from the stolen *Karaboudjan* flanked by Tom and Allan. His favorite car, the limousine he kept for special occasions, waited on the cobblestone quayside. Nestor stood by the passenger door, wearing his chauffeur's uniform. A locomotive belched steam and smoke nearby as the *Karaboudjan*'s regular cargo was unloaded onto the flatcars behind it. Everything was coming together despite that irritating urchin Tintin and the sot Haddock.

"What are we doing here, boss?" Tom asked as they

crossed the train tracks. An enormous crane swung over them to hoist pallets of cargo out of the *Karaboudjan*'s hold. There were several cranes nearby, on twenty-foot scaffolds bolted into platforms on the ground. "I don't get it. We're right back where we started."

"You're to speak of this to no one," Sakharine snapped. "Keep your mouths shut."

"Don't worry, long as we get our share," Allan said.

"Oh, you'll get your share," Sakharine said. He pointed back toward the gangplank. "Guard the ship."

Three scrolls in hand, Sakharine kept walking. Behind him, Tom kept complaining. "But where are you going? Where's the filthy moolah?"

You'll get just what you deserve, Sakharine thought. He left Tom and Allan where they stood and approached his car. Nestor opened the door. "Good evening, sir," he said. "I trust you had a successful trip abroad?"

"Do I pay you to talk to me?" Sakharine said. He got into the car. As Nestor shut the door after him, he heard him say, "You don't pay me at all."

Which was true enough, but Sakharine had more important things on his mind than the petty grumblings of his subordinates. He settled into the rich leather seat and focused his mind on the long-awaited conclusion to the quest for the secret of the *Unicorn*.

Then the car moved, but not forward.

Sakharine sat up. He looked out the window and saw to his astonishment that the car was rising into the air. "What the blazes?" he said. "Nestor!"

He rolled down the window and saw Tom and Allan running from the base of the gangway where he had stationed them, guns drawn. The car rose into the air, swinging gently, and Sakharine realized that one of the ship's large cranes had picked it up. "Tom, Allan, you blithering idiots, don't just stand there!" he screamed out the window. *"Do something!"*

Then, as the car swung around, Sakharine saw the accursed Captain Haddock in the cab of the crane controlling it...and singing one of his abominable songs as he worked the levers!

No, Sakharine thought. *It does not end like this.*

"You take the high road and I'll take the low road, and I'll be in Scotland before youuuuu..." Captain Haddock belted

the song out as he moved the car toward the roof of a building across the railroad tracks from the dock, where Tintin
waited with Thompson and Thomson.

Tintin almost had to laugh, listening. Something had
changed in the captain since the performance of the Milanese Nightingale and the flood. He was once again the for-
midable sea dog all his forebears had been. Tintin was
proud of him.

"Caught him like a rat in a trap," Thompson said next
to him.

"Congratulations, gentlemen," Tintin said. "He's all yours."

"Yes! We have warrants issued by both Interpol and the
FBI," Thomson said.

"Your friend who got shot on your doorstep," Thompson
began.

"Barnaby!?" Tintin exclaimed.

"One of their agents," Thompson admitted. "The FBI has
been hot on Sakharine's trail from the start."

"It still doesn't make any sense. He has the key to the
treasure of the *Unicorn*, which is sitting somewhere on the
ocean floor," Tintin wondered. "Why would he come back
home?"

Neither Thompson nor Thomson had an answer for this.

All three of them watched as Captain Haddock, laughing uproariously at some private joke, set the car down on the roof near them. Thompson stepped forward and opened the back door. "Right," he said. "Sakharine?"

The back of the car was empty.

All three of them crowded around the door in puzzlement. Then Sakharine shot up in the driver's seat, a gun in his hand. "That's *Mr.* Sakharine to you!" he said sharply, waving the gun to force them back.

They backed away. Tintin's mind raced. Sakharine couldn't imagine that he would escape even now, could he? He was stuck in a car on the end of a crane....

As he had the thought, the crane arm jerked wildly to the side and Sakharine's car swung toward them like a million-dollar wrecking ball. Tintin and the two detectives dove out of the way. The car slammed into a wall beyond them and then swung back before returning in another sweeping arc. It was out of control! Tintin heard a gunshot. He scrambled to the edge of the roof and looked down toward the crane cab.

Just as he had suspected, Allan and Captain Haddock were wrestling in the cab, and their actions had caused the crane arm's crazy swings. There was a bullet hole in one of the cab's windows. As Tintin watched, Haddock tumbled out of the cab and dangled from a railing at the edge. Allan got the crane under control and brought Sakharine's car smoothly off the roof.

But Captain Haddock wasn't done yet! He fought his way back into the cab and threw Allan out the other side. The thug fell into the bed of a passing truck, which screeched to a halt as its driver tried to figure out what had happened.

Sakharine's car had now swung across the tracks. As it came back, Sakharine flung open the car door and leaped over to another crane. He scrambled inside the cab, and the second crane's arm began to rise and angle toward Haddock's crane. It was like a sword fight, Tintin saw, only with ten-ton crane arms. The cranes collided with a deafening crash. Both operators, Sakharine and Captain Haddock, jostled and banged around inside their respective cabs. Sakharine's crane picked up a pallet of cement bags and threw them at Captain Haddock's cab. The impact swallowed Captain Haddock's cab in a cloud of cement dust. Snowy barked in frustration.

Captain Haddock kicked torn bags of cement out of his cab, frantically trying to clear his windshield. Sakharine struck again and Captain Haddock parried. The arm of

Sakharine's crane smashed through Captain Haddock's windshield. Captain Haddock hauled his crane arm up and to the side, tearing away the roof of Sakharine's cab.

His hair and beard flying as the cranes creaked and swayed on their scaffolds, Sakharine flung a pallet of the *Karaboudjan*'s cargo at the struts supporting Captain Haddock's crane. The boxes flew through the air, crashing and bouncing across the roof of the nearby building as Tintin, Snowy, and the detectives dodged and dived out of the way.

The fight went on between the cranes, which were battering each other to pieces. But now Sakharine's goons were on the roof, too. Tom was the first to appear, brandishing his gun, but three flying tires landed on him, pinning him to his spot. As more thugs raced to aid him, Snowy tugged a plank free from a crate of canned goods. The cans rolled out across the rooftop, tripping up the thugs and rattling among them as they fell.

The two cranes had now smashed in close to each other, their motors grinding as both Sakharine and Captain Haddock fought for leverage. "Red Rackham!" Captain Haddock growled.

"My ancestor," acknowledged Sakharine. "Just as Sir Francis was yours."

Captain Haddock forced his crane another inch forward. "Unfinished business," he said through gritted teeth.

"I'm glad you know the truth, Haddock," Sakharine said. "Until you could remember, killing you would not have been nearly this much fun!"

As he spoke, Sakharine pulled his crane backward, swinging its arm at the same time. The arm crashed into Captain Haddock's crane and knocked it over sideways. It toppled slowly, crashing onto the deck of the *Karaboudjan*. Cement dust drifted over the deck, reminding Tintin of the smoke from gunpowder and broken lanterns. Captain Haddock scrambled free of the wreckage.

Cool and calm, Sakharine lowered his crane arm to the deck and then walked down it as Captain Haddock caught his breath. "Who gave you permission to board my ship?" Captain Haddock said.

Sakharine grinned wickedly. "I don't need it," he said, whipping out his sword cane. "I never needed it."

Captain Haddock grabbed a broken control lever from the crane cab. Sakharine lunged, and the battle was joined in hand-to-hand combat. They fought as only ancient enemies can fight, but Captain Haddock fought fair, and this was his undoing. Sakharine deflected one of his attacks and kicked his legs out from under him. As Captain Haddock struggled back to his feet, Sakharine flung a fishnet over him, then ripped it away, sending Captain Haddock spinning across the deck and crashing into a crate that had fallen from one of the cranes.

On his hands and knees, Captain Haddock saw a bottle of whiskey roll across the deck in front of him. He looked up. Sakharine was walking away.

Oh, no, you don't, thought Captain Haddock. *Not just yet.*

Tintin cheered and Snowy barked from the rooftop as Captain Haddock bombarded Sakharine with bottles. Some of them broke on the deck around him. Others hit Sakharine's body, making him stagger. Sakharine ducked for cover and fell from the main deck onto a lower platform at the side of the ship — not far from where Tintin had made his daring climb from porthole to porthole when the *Kara-boudjan* was on the high seas.

Captain Haddock came to the railing, one bottle held in his hand, ready to end things once and for all.

But Sakharine rolled over and came to his feet with the scrolls in one hand ... and a lighter in the other!

"The legend says only a Haddock can discover the secret of the *Unicorn*," sneered Sakharine. "But it took a Rackham to get the job done! You've lost again, Haddock. Why don't you have a drink? That's all you've got left. Everything that was yours is now mine. Including this ship!"

Captain Haddock saw red. He leaped over the railing, plummeting toward the platform where Sakharine stood — and at the same time Tintin swung in on one of the crane cables and snatched the scrolls from Sakharine's hand. "Thundering typhoons!" Captain Haddock roared. He punched Sakharine so hard that the master thief did a backward somersault down into the water.

"Nobody takes my ship!" Captain Haddock yelled after him, throwing the last bottle. It hit Sakharine squarely on top of the head.

Tintin had landed on one of the upper railings along the side of the *Karaboudjan*'s superstructure. Captain Haddock looked up and they locked eyes. They both nodded.

It took only a few moments for Thompson and Thomson to commandeer a local police boat and pull the battered Sakharine out of the water. "We have you now, you devil!" Thompson said. "You are under arrest."

"To be precise," Thomson corrected him, "you are under arrest."

Sakharine looked from one to the other as if he wasn't quite certain that he had heard them correctly. Finally, he raised his hands in defeat.

The sun was just coming up. It was a new day.

Tintin and Captain Haddock watched the police boat motor away with the resigned and drenched Sakharine handcuffed on its deck. What a story this was going to be! Tintin thought. And it just kept getting better and better.

He looked out over the harbor at the sun, which had risen high enough for his purposes.

"Captain," he said. Haddock looked over, squinting against the sunlight. Tintin held up the scrolls, overlapping the edges so the sun shone through all three at once. Captain Haddock shifted so the light wasn't directly in his eyes, and the two of them looked closely at the scrolls. Tintin heard Snowy's nails clicking up the gangway. Everyone was present for this final revelation.

"Do you see?" Tintin said. He pointed to a row of numbers and letters along the bottom of all three scrolls.

"Blistering barnacles!" cried Captain Haddock. "They're coordinates!"

Nodding, Tintin said, "It took all three scrolls to form the numbers."

Captain Haddock's finger traced the symbols. "Latitude

and longitude..." he murmured. "That's it! That's the location of the treasure."

He caught Tintin's hand, and the two of them danced around the deck laughing like maniacs. "We did it!" they shouted, over and over. Snowy danced around with them, barking with joy.

They wasted no time getting a jeep and heading out of town and into the countryside, with Captain Haddock peering through a sextant as though they were navigating on the high seas. "Almost there, Mr. Tintin," he said, standing on the passenger seat as the wind blasted through his beard. "A nudge to starboard should do it."

"Are you sure we're on course?" Tintin asked. They bounced down a dirt road in the middle of nowhere.

"Aye, trust me, laddie," Captain Haddock said. "I know these parts like the back of my hand."

Tintin looked around. He wasn't sure, but he thought Captain Haddock might have been bluffing, just a little.

"Starboard! Quickly!" Captain Haddock cried, still peering through the sextant.

"Aye, Captain, starboard it is!" Tintin said, turning the

jeep sharply to the right. They went off the road immediately and crashed through a line of hedges before bouncing across a meadow and jolting up onto the driveway of Marlinspike Hall!

"Full stop!" yelled Captain Haddock as the jeep's front tires banged into Marlinspike Hall's front steps.

Tintin turned off the engine, and they both looked up, not quite believing what they were seeing. "Marlinspike Hall," Captain Haddock breathed.

"Those coordinates led here. This is where Sir Francis hid it?" Tintin was confused. He ran through everything they had learned. What had he missed? "I thought the treasure went down with the ship."

The door opened and Nestor appeared. "Master Haddock," he said. "Master Tintin. I've been expecting you."

Captain Haddock and Tintin looked at each other. Things were getting stranger by the minute. But they got out of the jeep and walked up to the door, Snowy trotting along just behind.

"Welcome to Marlinspike Hall," Nestor said as they entered.

"Would you look at this place!" Captain Haddock exulted. "I don't think it's changed at all since I was a wee boy."

"And may I say, sir, how much I am looking forward to

having a Haddock back in charge of the estate." Nestor bowed.

"You'll be waiting a long time, Nestor," Captain Haddock said wistfully. "There's no way I could afford to live here."

For a moment they stood in the grand foyer looking around. Tintin had only been inside at night, and had been woozy from Nestor rapping him over the head with a candlestick, so he saw it as if for the first time. It was easy to see how magnificent Marlinspike Hall had once been. The floor was polished marble and the main entry stairway rails were hand-carved. Tapestries and paintings that must have been priceless decorated the walls—including, Tintin saw, a portrait of Sir Francis himself hanging in a sitting room visible from just inside the front door. Other arched doorways opened into dim rooms decorated in the understated style of old money. All Marlinspike Hall needed, Tintin thought, was someone living there who cared about its history. Perhaps Captain Haddock would be that person...if they could find the treasure.

That thought brought Tintin back to the present, and to the story! Where was the treasure? Which way should they explore first? There were more stairways and corridors leading away than they could explore in a week. "Well, Captain, you know the house," Tintin said. "Where do we start?"

The guard dog that had chased Tintin all over the grounds on his last visit trotted out of an interior room and woofed, wagging the stub of its tail. Snowy trotted up to it, and they circled and sniffed. Captain Haddock squinted as if his memories of Marlinspike Hall were faint and hard to read. Then he turned to Nestor. "Is the cellar still here?"

Nestor led them down a curving stone staircase into a vaulted cellar packed with the trophies and heirlooms of generations of Haddocks. Tintin's pulse quickened. Surely this was it!

But Captain Haddock looked around in confusion. "No, no, no," he muttered. Turning to Nestor, he said, "This isn't it. I meant the other cellar."

"I'm sorry, sir?" Nestor looked puzzled. "There is no other cellar."

"It was bigger than this," Captain Haddock said. He reached out and touched one wall, looking around as if trying to place himself on a map in his head.

Tintin looked around, too, and noticed that Snowy was gone. He didn't want any expensive antiques chewed up or knocked over. "Snowy?" he called. "Captain, have you seen him?"

Captain Haddock was still locked in his reverie; but the guard dog suddenly made a beeline for a stack of shrouded furniture. It lowered its head and scratched at the base of the wall. Tintin came up next to the hound and peered through the sheets covering the furniture. There appeared to be a small opening in the wall. "Snowy?" Tintin called. He thought he heard an answering bark. "Captain, help me."

Nestor and Captain Haddock helped Tintin shift the furniture aside, exposing the hole in the wall. Tintin looked at Captain Haddock and saw that they were thinking the same thing: Someone must have walled off part of the cellar, which would explain why Captain Haddock remembered a larger area.

Snowy whined eagerly. "Just like you said, Captain," Tintin said, remembering their conversation on the beach after the flood, when things seemed at their most hopeless. "You hit a wall..."

"You push through it!" Captain Haddock finished.

They looked around and found an old timber lying along the base of the wall nearby. Picking it up and aiming it at the edge of the small opening, they used it as a battering ram. *Boom!* At the first impact, bricks and stones fell away, tripling the size of the hole. Tintin set down his end of the timber and got on his hands and knees to pick through the rubble. He discovered a long, vaulted room, lit by small skylights that must have been angled cleverly at different parts of the house's roof. The room was lined with paintings, statues, suits of armor . . . it was a treasure trove of souvenirs from around the world! Statues of Egyptian gods and Buddhas sat surrounded by open chests and crates filled to overflowing with trinkets and mementoes of generations of Haddocks and all their voyages across all the world's oceans. Flags of long-vanished nations hung from the ceiling, or from the points of ceremonial spears. On one wall, a row of masks looked down like a gallery of ancient spectators waiting to see what show Tintin might perform. He stood stunned for a moment, taking it all in.

Captain Haddock had come through the hole in the wall right behind Tintin. "My grandfather must have walled it up before he lost the house," he said, walking deeper into the hidden space. He picked up an ancient cap-and-ball pistol and hefted it as if it were familiar to him. Then, setting it down, he flipped through a leather-bound book filled with angular cursive. A diary of one of his forebears, Tintin thought. Captain Haddock was home.

But Marlinspike Hall wouldn't really be his home unless they found the treasure. Captain Haddock kept picking things up and putting them down again. There was so much to look at! They searched through the room as Tintin thought about the next clue in the scrolls.

"And then shines forth the Eagle's Cross..." he quoted.

They didn't see an eagle anywhere. "I can see the cross," Captain Haddock said, pointing at a statue of a man holding a cross, "but where's the eagle?"

Tintin looked closely at the statue. "St. John the Evangelist!" he said. "He was called the Eagle of Patmos. He's the eagle...." But that wasn't all they needed to know. Where did the cross shine forth? Why? "But what is he trying to tell us, Captain? I'm at a loss."

They stepped back to get a little perspective, looking up and down the shadowed walls. Tintin noticed that the cross St. John held gleamed a little in the pale shafts of light that fell from the ceiling. He had a thought. "Captain, look," he said.

He reached out and held a hand in front of the cross, blocking whatever light it might reflect. Captain Haddock pointed. "There," he said. Tintin moved his hand again and reflected light fell on a carved stone globe across the room from the statue.

Looking closely at it, Tintin saw no clues. It was a beautiful globe, no question about it. But it was just a globe, with carved reliefs of various island chains and coastlines.

"That island," Captain Haddock said, pointing. "The one in the middle. That doesn't exist."

Amazed, Tintin looked from the globe to Captain Haddock. "How do you know?"

"Because I've sailed those waters countless times. I've been there," Captain Haddock said. "It's a mistake."

Now Tintin felt the thrill, the quickening of his pulse and his thoughts, that he always experienced when he knew he was right on the verge of a big story. A huge story. "What if it isn't?" he asked.

"Isn't what?" Captain Haddock said.

"A mistake. Sir Francis wanted his inheritance to go to a man who was worthy of it," Tintin said. "A man like himself, who knows the seas like the back of his hand. A man who could look at a globe and tell if one tiny island was out of place."

Captain Haddock caught his breath. A slow grin stole over his face. Tintin nodded at him, encouraging him.

Captain Haddock reached out slowly and with one finger-tip pressed on the island that shouldn't have been there....

There was a soft click, and the top of the globe—from the Arctic Circle northward—lifted open like a lid.

Tintin and Captain Haddock leaned forward and peered into the globe, not daring to hope.

"Blistering treasure," Captain Haddock said quietly. "It's Red Rackham's barnacles!"

Tintin laughed and reached into the globe. When he pulled his hand out, it was filled with the warm glow of gold pieces and the sharp glitter of cut jewels. He couldn't believe it. Red Rackham's treasure!

"What's this?" Captain Haddock said as he reached in himself. He stood and removed an old felt tricorne. Tintin recognized it immediately from Captain Haddock's stories. It was Sir Francis's own hat, and it was filled with more treasure. With a delighted laugh, Captain Haddock spilled everything into a nearby box and put the hat on. He sighed, and Tintin wished he had a camera. This was the moment, he thought, when Captain Haddock assumed his birthright.

But there was more! At the bottom of the globe lay another piece of parchment.

Tintin was about to look at it when Nestor arrived

bearing a tray with a bottle of champagne and a pair of glasses. He set down the tray and regarded the scene. Tintin thought he looked satisfied. Nestor had been on their side all along, he thought; he would have to make sure to tell everyone that when it was time to get this story out.

"Aahhhhhh," Captain Haddock said. "A wee tipple, a toast to good fortune." He drank his glass and looked thoughtful for a moment. "It's odd, really. After all the fuss and bother, you'd have thought there would be more."

"More of what?" Tintin asked as Captain Haddock drank Tintin's glass of champagne, too.

"Red Rackham's treasure," Captain Haddock said. "I mean, by your own account he looted half of South America! I just thought...well, never mind. There's plenty to go around." Again he grew thoughtful, and Tintin became more and more curious about what was in his mind. "It's a funny old life," Captain Haddock said. "You've got your story for your newspaper. All's well that ends well."

Tintin was sorry to see Captain Haddock disappointed. There was one more thing he wanted to tell the captain, but he didn't want to say it when anyone else was around. Tintin had not forgotten that, until yesterday, Nestor had been in Sakharine's employ. He waited until Nestor had gathered up the champagne glasses and left. Then he said quietly, "It's not ended." Captain Haddock looked up from a bauble in his hand, and Tintin showed him the parchment. It was a map. "Sir Francis left another clue at the bottom of the globe."

"A clue to what?" Captain Haddock asked eagerly.

"Four hundred weight of gold, just lying at the bottom of the sea," Tintin said. "How's your thirst for adventure, Captain?"

Surrounded by the wealth of his ancestors, Captain Haddock suddenly looked like he could conquer the world. "Unquenchable, Tintin!" he said.

Mine, too, Tintin thought. He could already feel the thrill of the new adventure that awaited them. Captain Haddock resettled Sir Francis's hat on his head and leaned in close so he could get a good look at the map Tintin held.

"Blistering barnacles," Captain Haddock said. "Four hundred weight of gold, just waiting for us to find it."

Snowy put his paws up on Tintin's lap, took one look at the map, and barked.

"That's right, Snowy," Tintin said. "We may not have told the whole story just yet."

THE END